The Salvation of Nino Strata

A Novel

I0554051

Christian Colossus

DEDICATION

I dedicate this book to the three persons of the Holy Trinity.

The first person is God the Father, who is Almighty God, the eternal Lord, Yahweh; and my Heavenly Father.

The second person is God the Son, my Lord and Savior, Yahshua ha'Mashiah aka Jesus Christ.

The third person is God the Holy Spirit, my Holy Guide and Comforter. You never leave me nor forsake me.

To all three of you, I can never say thank you enough. And once again I say, "Thank You," forever more.

I also dedicate this book to my dear friend, Anthony. The Lord used you to minister to me at an important time in my life. You are a friend, brother, helper and counselor. Wherever you are, I say, "Thank You," for everything.

TABLE OF CONTENTS

The color of true power is the highest heaven,
And the beauty of the rainbow is varied in seven.
The color of human love is unique to every heart,
And the success of destiny is at its end not its start.
The color of wisdom is the excellence of its choices,
And trouble is known by its strange and evil voices.
The color of human madness is the barrel of a gun,
And red is the blood when the madness is done.
The color of God's love is in human salvation,
And yellow are the rays of the golden sun.

"Yellow Are the Rays of the Golden Sun"
—Christian Colossus

PROLOGUE

Yellow Are the Rays of the Golden Sun

The winds blew very strongly, but they didn't blow in any specific direction just rotating around any object in their path. These were strong circling whirlwinds, the most special kind of winds given the occasion. They also had the features of the most special kinds of winds—heavenly whirlwinds. Neither sun nor moon shone here, but that couldn't be noticed as the light that lit up the kingdom was everywhere. It was not only dazzling, but it was also a brilliant and breathtaking shade of white. It was the most beautiful white light that there ever was and on reaching any hard surface scattered into the colors of the visible spectrum. The color, intensity, and brilliance of the light were soothing, overpowering and indicative of the sheer beauty of the great majesty from which it drew its source. There was no night and no day but a constant and pure glowing shine that seemed to come from everywhere. Beautiful white and multi-colored birds filled the heavens. They had no worries as they flew the length and breadth of the skies. One city joined to another in an endless union like a glittering string of priceless jewels. The rivers, mountains, hills and other parts of the topography were all beautiful and perfect in their shapes, flow and appearance. The trees, flowers, fruit and all the other vegetation sang a song that glorified the majesty of the king of this great kingdom. In the northern end of the kingdom shone the brightest of the lights that radiated throughout the kingdom. Suddenly, a great man appeared from the northern region of the kingdom flying on great clouds through the skies approaching one of the great mountains in the east of the kingdom. The man wore white robes, holding a golden spear in his right hand and seemed to be in a bit of a hurry. He just received commandment from the almighty King to carry out right away. He arrived at the summit of the great mountain and he set his feet down quickly on the stones of the mountains. As he did so, the cloud of transportation that brought him disappeared for a moment. His height was about 300 feet and had a rounded face with black hair and fiery eyes which looked downward from the edge of the east as he stood on the mountains. His eyes were roving to and fro looking down at the structures far beneath the kingdom until his eyes located the oval yellowish disk that shone with great intensity. Smaller oval bodies rotated around this yellow disk and surrounded it. The great man pointed one end of the golden spear at the sun and a flash like lightning left the spear and rushed towards the sun. As the flash struck the sun, a small explosion occurred and the great noise coming from the sun mellowed down for a moment. As this happened the man on the mountain shouted at the top of his voice words that the yellow sun seemed to hear and understand.

"O thou sun, listen and hearken to the words of your Creator, and fulfill the will of the hands that formed you which has sent me to instruct you. Turn your great rays unto the favored continent that lies between the great oceans in the middle of the South of the earth. Now you shall sow the earth in this continent and the waters close to the earth with gold from your rays, so that the gold shall be abundant and of great quality. And let this gold fill the earth and under the waters that pass through this continent, greater in the South but lesser in the

North. And let the nations reap this treasure that they may become great and fulfill the will of the Highest. For yellow are the rays of the golden sun."

As soon as the man finished speaking these words, he withdrew his spear and placed it by his side. He then focused his gaze on the sun. After his words ended, the man continued to look at the sun. The sun projected its rays towards the northern and southern hemisphere and unto a particular continent. Soon a river bisected this continent and ran its course from the North Atlantic Ocean to the South Atlantic Ocean. The sun's rays remained focused on this continent for about ten minutes. And then the sun withdrew its rays back to itself. The man on the mountain then mounted similar clouds which transported him to the mountain and flew on the clouds back towards the northern region of the kingdom.

****

The continent of Yellow River got its name from the vast extent of the great river of the same name traversing the length of the continent. Yellow River began from the great ocean, the North Atlantic Ocean, and ran a course southward traversing the nations of the continent. It passed through the four regions which made up the continent directly or via its vast tributaries. Those tributaries coursed through every nation on the continent and emptied countless gallons every minute into the gigantic river. There were the northern, eastern, southern and western regional subcontinents. The various regional subcontinents each had either three or four countries comprising that region. The southern subcontinent comprised four different countries, of which Cretania was one of them. Both the southern and northern subcontinents each had four countries. The eastern and western subcontinents both had three countries each. Nations of the southern regional subcontinent aligned one after the other in a horizontal pattern. In the South, the four nations were Atlantis, Cretania, Calamus and Corona running from east to west. And in the North, the four nations were Normarin, Quartos, Quintos and Brooklyn going from east to west. Quintos and Quartos had the Yellow River passing between them and separating them. Both nations had the river as their common border on the East and the West respectively, as the river passed through the northern subcontinent. And from there the river entered the nation of Cretania snaking through the nation and dividing that nation into West and East with almost perfect symmetry. The nations of Quartos and Quintos formed the northeastern and northwestern borders of Cretania, respectively. The great river ended by emptying itself through its mouth into the South Atlantic Ocean. By this course it created a complex waterway linking the waters of the North Atlantic in the North to the South Atlantic in the South.

The eastern subcontinent of Yellow River had three nations arranged in an almost vertical structure. They were Linmarin, Estus and Maximus running from north to south. Linmarin was bordered in the North by Normarin while its southern border was Estus. Maximus was located between Estus in the north and northeast Atlantis in the south. All the eastern nations were bordered on the east by the joint Atlantic Ocean. And on the west, the eastern subcontinent was bordered by the eastern border of the nations of the western regional subcontinent.

Continental Yellow River's western subcontinent comprised of three nations namely Veritas, Cascade and Westbrook running from north to south. Veritas' northeastern border was the North Atlantic Ocean and Brooklyn. Its southern border was the nation of Cascade. Cascade was bordered by Veritas in the north and Westbrook in the south. Westbrook was bordered in the North by Cascade and in the South by Corona and the South Atlantic Ocean. The North and South Atlantic Oceans formed the western border of the western subcontinent. The nations of the eastern subcontinent formed the eastern border of the nations of the western regional subcontinent.

The river, Yellow, was the primary artery that ran through and fed the whole of the Cretanian nation. The passage of Yellow River through Cretania created twelve states with six on each side of an almost perfect symmetry. On the east side running from south to north were the states of Eastern River, Happyness, Portland, Communitas, South Atlantis and North Atlantis. On the western side of the divide running in the same order from south to north, the states of Western River, Calazar, Shiloh, Prophétie, South Capitol and North Capitol. The capital of the nation was the city of Crestar, a city designed to have an equal amount of real estate between both North and South Capitol on their eastern borders where they meet with the Yellow River. North Capitol City and South Capitol City served as the capital cities of the corresponding states. The two Capitol cities formed a triangle with the national capital. The national capital was the top of this triangle with the left lower point being the capital of Northern Capitol. And the right lower point was the capital city of South Capitol. The capitals of the eastern states were Mint City in the northeastern part of Eastern River and the city of Joy in the southcentral region of Happyness. The city of Ferry Run, the capital of Portland, was in the center of the western region of Portland at the state border with the Yellow River. Commune City, capital of Communitas, was in the southeast of Communitas. The capitals of South Atlantis and North Atlantis were Atlantis City in northcentral South Atlantis and New Atlantis in northwestern North Atlantis. The capital cities of the western states were the city of Westania in the central region of Western River and the city of Summit in the northern region of Calazar. The capitals of Shiloh and Prophétie were the cities of Shiloh in the central region of Shiloh State and Bethel City in the center of southern Prophétie, respectively. Crestar City, the national capital, was located at the boundaries between South Capitol and North Capitol at their borders with Yellow River. As a whole, the country's size equaled 850,000 square miles with the States of Happyness, Western River, Eastern River and Calazar having the largest sizes. The states of North Capitol, South Capitol, Communitas and Portland had the smallest geographical sizes.

Cretania's economy was the strongest in the continent. It was the only nation in Yellow River that had sustained an economy which was in the top fifteen of all the nations of the world. Some nations never received that distinction while other nations rose to levels as high as the top twenty in the world. But most of them could not sustain an economy at such high levels of growth, development and Gross Domestic Product. The strong Cretanian economy received large contribution from the economics of its huge gold reserves. Low production costs and high sales price characterized the economics of gold in the commodity markets. The relatively inexpensive gold production resulted from the abundance of gold and the ease of its mining in Cretania. Cretania earned the name of 'Goldenville' in the Western hemisphere due to its abundant gold. With its GDP just a fraction shy of 1.95 trillion cretari, the Cretanian economy was not only strong, but it had a great future ahead of it. Also, not only was gold abundant but successive governments had created laws that ensured there will never be a monopoly in the mining and distribution of gold. The same laws applied to other aspects of the supply chain that provided Cretanian gold to the world markets. Well-capitalized businesses could go into the gold mining and production business. But it was not only the gold that made the country so wealthy. Cretania had abundant amounts of crude oil, diamonds and other precious stones. The most abundant precious stones besides diamonds were aquamarine, topaz, chrysolite, amethyst and sapphire. But gold was the most abundant of all natural resources with its reserves reaching as much as half to three-fifths of global reserves. The strong economy reflected in the strength of the country's official currency—the Cretanian 'cretarius'—which was about 150% of the value of one American dollar. Thus, one million cretari was equivalent to 1.5 million US dollars. The low inflation numbers never rose above the average found in the subcontinent and the continent as a whole. Interest rates never rose higher than 2% except in the very rarest of cases and foreign direct investment was very high. The nation's sovereign wealth fund boasted 7.5% of GDP because many past governments invested the national assets wisely. Cretania was a modern developed country, what many economists would call a "first-world country." The Bank of Cretania, the country's central bank, always reported a strong healthy economy to the financial world including global financial institutions.

The climate of the continent of Yellow River was a cross between a tropical and a temperate one. With the southern nations having a more tropical climate, the northern nations had more of a temperate climate. But even in the warmest countries, like those in the South of the southern subcontinent such as Cretania, it was usual for some states to experience the four seasons typical of temperate regions. The northern states of North and South Atlantis, North and South Capitol and Prophétie had such weather. But where Cretania differed from other nations like Calamus was that most of its northern states had cities with elevations as high as 2000 feet above sea level. It was this feature that conferred on them mountainous climates. Mountainous and high-elevation states like Calazar, Shiloh, Prophétie and North and South Capitol commonly had elevations exceeding 4000 feet above sea level. Calamus, on the other hand, had low elevations with the highest being about 400 feet above sea level.

The population of Cretania was a balanced mix in the sense that most races and nationalities of the world were represented in the country. The golden years of prosperity that the country enjoyed began during the days of the work of the missionaries in the country. It was this prosperity that attracted migrants from all parts of the world who were looking to partake in the prosperity by filling the many vacant job positions. These people joined in the rush of extracting the various mineral ores from the earth. These migrants made their living by working in the mines or selling mining equipment to the miners. And after retiring from working the mines, they would retire and settle in one of the many serene cities in the country. Other migrants migrated to the country for the sake of settling down in a stable, well-developed democracy. The main tribes and races in Cretania were the Western Europeans, Jews from all tribes of Israel, Southern Africans and Eastern Africans especially Ethiopians. There were also the Western Africans, Chinese, Japanese, Americans, Canadians and Middle Eastern Arabs. The minor groups included Eastern Europeans, Lebanese and Russians. The first settlers were the Southern and Western Africans but they were few in numbers and they lived in sparsely populated communal settlements. Then the missionaries from America and Western Europe arrived and as they went about spreading the gospel, they discovered vast mineral resources which they mined. All proceeds of the wealth produced from the mines was shared with the locals, if any, and used to develop the communities. The greatest amount of ore found was the precious metal, gold, and the deposits were not only found inland but also on the seashore and in the sea. This mineral was so vast and plentiful throughout the continent it was often considered the cause of the yellow discoloration observed in some of the rivers and waterways. Soon, this main river that crisscrossed the nation almost bifurcating the country into equal halves was given the name it bears till this day. The missionaries who arrived in great numbers saw this as a sign that God Almighty had destined this country for greatness and for the residence of his people. Many of the missionaries invited their families to join them. Soon, word of the large deposits of gold and other minerals reached the outside world. This triggered a rush by migrants and even more missionaries into the country. That was about 150 years ago and by now most citizens had become a mixture of the various nationalities and races that settled in the country over the decades. Most newborn citizens of Cretania, about 70%, descended from mixed nationality, race and tribe. Only about 30% of the citizenry were of the same race, tribe or national background. This was because of their birth by parents whose ancestors by choice or otherwise married from the same nationality, race or tribe.

All peoples were invited as long as they lived and abided by the laws of the country as written in the constitution. That document was drafted by the leaders of the day who were all Christian. They worked with the finest constitution lawyers who were themselves Christians and were well versed in their field. The implementation, and enforcement, of the laws was very strict and all violators paid heavy penalties. The intention was the same as always — to deter others from criminal behavior and disregarding the laws of the land. The leaders chose constitutional democracy as their system of government. Those who drafted the constitution were forty-nine in number with four from each state and one presiding as Speaker of the House of Parliament to oversee the activities of the House of Parliament. The first national leader was a prime minister who was a member of the parliament. He was chosen because he was the leader of the largest of all the political parties in the House of Parliament. It was a constitutional parliamentary system and it worked quite well. At least it worked as long as the great Christian leaders who founded the country were alive to administer and lead the people of the country. The primary mistake of the founding fathers was the belief that migrants would accept, and live by, the godly ways of Cretania. That strategy turned out to be a terrible error of judgment.

As time went on, a massive dilution of the population occurred due to over-migration, and cracks appeared in the wall. The reasons for the cracks became quite obvious as the population grew from 5 million during the days of the founding fathers to about 60 million, just about 150 years later. First, many of the great leaders who built the empire did not have any designated successors who were as devoted as they were to godliness and holiness. Second, the generosity of the great leaders would become their main undoing. The flawed system of letting anyone come in as long as they vowed to always abide by the laws of godliness once they entered the country showed its terrible weaknesses. Many of those who came from religious backgrounds violated their vows of adhering to laws of godliness. These detractors set up worship houses to worship and serve their own gods. It was only a matter of time before full-fledged idolatry flourished and this led to other sins. Eventually, the forbidden sins began to raise their ugly heads. And, by the time these ungodly behaviors occurred, there were all kinds of sins in the land. But unfortunately the great leaders who would have confronted and destroyed these evils had all died. And there wasn't a new crop of great leaders to prevent these unholy changes. In time, the 'lambs' had been surrounded by 'wolves.' And after 150 years, it took the cries of the old guard before they died to move the almighty hand. And that move was to initiate the restoration of the 'beautiful country' back to its original glory. The few remaining prophets stood on the old promises made to their ancestors by their God a long time ago.

The Cretanian infrastructure was one of the most developed and most sophisticated of any country in the continent. Due to its strong economy, the country attracted high-quality talent, products, and services. The transportation network comprised extensive road, air and rail networks. There were four main North-South road arterial networks — two of them ran from north to south in the eastern and western parts of the country. The eastern North-South highway was Interstate Highway 7 while the western highway was Interstate Highway 14. There were seven East-West arterial networks with three major ones and four minor ones and each one having a section that crosses the Yellow River at various points. They all ran their courses traversing an east-to-west direction through different states. The first of the major networks ran from the southern parts of Happyness to Calazar and it was called the 'Chappy' aka EW3. Another major one ran to northern Shiloh from northern Communitas and was called 'Coshi' aka EW2. The largest major network ran to North Capitol from North Atlantic and was called 'Norcat' aka EW1. Many cities had well-developed subway systems which supported the economic, geopolitical and infrastructural development of those cities and surrounding areas. All major cities, including all state capitals, had international airports. Most cities had well-developed subway and surface rail networks. Cretania's technology infrastructure and InfoTech systems never scored below the highest score, AAA, for 45 years in a row. The country's technology sector was by far the most advanced in the continent.

Most cities boasted large hospitals, whether general, specialist or teaching hospitals. Some cities like the capital cities of the states usually boasted of one or more of these hospitals. Health care didn't come cheap in Cretania and every state took care of the health of its residents. There was no universal health care as that had been defeated in the federal legislature when the bill came up for voting. Universal health care which once existed in some states were all canceled except for the state of Prophétie. There was no universal care but the health care was heavily subsidized by the wealthy corporations, faith-based and charitable organizations headquartered in the state. The state of Prophétie had many distinctions that distinguished it from all the other states. Health insurance in the state cost as little as 50 cretari per year for those who made any income below a certain threshold. It was free for those who had no income or who had financial hardship or were disabled in any way. The state was also the 'home of the prophets' and about 85% to 90% of Cretanian prophets lived in the state. And one mysterious thing that happened once people were given the 'prophetic' title was that they would gravitate towards the state of Prophétie soon. A popular rumor had it that once a person moved to live in the state, the anointing of prophecy would come upon those true to the faith. The state of Prophétie used to be known as the home of the French-speaking missionaries. And here the vast majority of the French-speaking people of Cretania live even until this day. In the days when the missionaries arrived in the country, they set up their church branches in the region. The main reason may have been because of the mountainous topography in the state. With time, every missionary who spoke the French language as their mother tongue or as a secondary language ended up in the state. The early settlers had built institutions and organizations which provided services in French and this became the strongest reason for anyone who spoke French to make Prophétie their home. At the creation of the nation, they had opted to have French included as the second official language besides English.

All the states had political legislatures that comprised people who the state residents voted into office as it was done in any democracy. It was true for all the states, except for the state of Prophétie. In the state, the Council of Elders, which comprised the wisest and highest-ranking Christian elders, would cast lots for those to hold office in the legislature. The state of Prophétie was the only state with no history of electoral issues in the country. In the federal elections, all states would vote for their electoral choices and all voting was digital with the results available within seven hours after the end of voting.

The educational system and infrastructure was very advanced as the country had very reliable primary, secondary and tertiary institutions; and many of them ranked as some of the best in the world. About seven decades ago, the government of President Veracious Chen set out to revamp the educational system of the country and he came out with laws that overhauled the existing educational system. Every state had to have at least seven institutions of higher learning with at least one of them being focused on technology and other great academic disciplines. There had to be at least three of those schools with all the professional schools known to education including schools of medicine, dentistry, pharmacy, veterinary medicine and others. And every school of medicine must build a teaching hospital to accompany the medical school, in order to have well-trained physicians and surgeons. At first, the new laws were seen as draconian by the educational sector but with great determination the government made it work. States with the highest population of intellectuals, organizations and corporations such as Shiloh, Prophétie, Calazar, Happyness, Portland and North Capitol were the first to achieve the goals of the Chen government. Shiloh achieved the goal in about 15 years with Calazar doing same about three years later and Prophétie about two years after Calazar State. By the 50th year, every state in the country had achieved those goals and the nation's educational system suddenly transformed into one of the best in the world. Seventy years after President's Chen educational transformation began, the results were amazing. Cretania's top five universities—the University of Shiloh, Shiloh City, Caplon University, Turban University, SET University and

Calazar Institute of Technology—ranked in the top twenty listing of universities in the world. The University of Shiloh, Shiloh City was ranked third for the third year running and the Calazar Institute of Technology ranked at number seven.

At the time of the fight for nationhood, the men who had settled in the region joined to make demands on the corporate interests of powerful nations doing business in the region. They demanded all nations and companies involved in mining and other economic activities to concede to the settlers for nation formation. At first, they refused but the struggle that ensued ended with a few concessions so that the founding fathers came together to form a nation. The most influential group of those who struggled to gain the rights to form a nation was led by Antonius Alessandro Kriti. He was a Greek merchant and missionary who came to the region from the Greek Island of Crete. His struggle lasted till the day he died and cost him many friends, relatives and nearly his own life. In honor of his brave struggle the founding fathers called the nation 'Cretania.'

But things changed for worse over the past few decades. As governments led by members of clandestine societies came to power, the economy now charted a downward trend. And it was not just the economy but every aspect of Cretanian society seemed to be regressing rather than progressing. As more and more immigrants came and settled in the country, the strong morale and discipline eroded over time. These factors conspired to induce the decadence found in every aspect of Cretanian society. From educational honesty to political integrity to sexual chastity, everything suffered a sure and steady decline. It is this troubling state of affairs that witnessed the birth of the fourth generation of citizens in the post-creation period of Cretania.

CHAPTER ONE

The Beginning

Benjamin Strata and his wife Maraya was a married couple who lived in the affluent neighborhood of York in the city of Shiloh, the financial capital of the nation of Cretania. Benjamin was forty years old and his wife was five years younger. They had met twenty years before in the University of Shiloh, Shiloh City when he was a student studying chemical engineering and she was studying molecular biology. It was the night of matriculation and they both attended the party thrown by one of their common friends who was also studying engineering. They continued to run into each other around the campus; because the faculties of engineering and life sciences were side by side and they had common electives together. In their second year, they dated and immediately noticed they shared many things in common. Like many Cretanians, Benjamin had mixed heritage but Maraya was from a Southern African tribe on both sides of her ancestry. His mother was from the tribe of *Itombi*, which was the same tribe of Maraya's parents. Mr. Strata's paternal ancestry was American Caucasian and his father's ancestors had come to the country as a builder of churches and schools for the missionaries. That was over 100 years ago and they stayed, got married and raised their families in the country. Benjamin and Maraya both hated religion and they vowed they would have nothing to do with it. But there was one thing they found about each other that sealed the deal.

In the eastern end of the university there was a large farm owned by the university. It had all kinds of fruits and vegetables. In the deepest part of the farm there was a strange plantation in which seemed to grow strange trees. In that part of the farm there was a stern warning posted around there warning people not to enter that area. *Area X*, as it was known, was rumored to be the meeting place of all the witches and wizards in the university community and its environs. One night there was a loud beating of drums and other sounds coming from the farm. Those who were familiar knew what was going on. It was the night of meeting on the new moon. It was 'Matriculation Night' in the university's dark world. All the dark souls began arriving in the pitch-black plantation around midnight. Benjamin and Maraya had arrived at different times with their friends who knew about this university tradition. All those who were new to such a meeting were summoned up to the high table to introduce themselves to the people. On the high table were the leadership of the university and they were in charge of the coven. A group of ladies were the first to get to the high table and they introduced themselves to the other people. They told them their names, courses of study, ethnicities and other information about themselves. When the tenth lady introduced herself, Benjamin screamed with excitement, immediately left his friends and ran towards the high table. It was Maraya Nestel, his new found crush and sweetheart. As Maraya saw Benjamin coming she flew from the high table all the way into his open hands. "Maraya, you are here, you are a woman of power. Thank God," he whispered into her ears. "You too, my dear Benji, I can't believe it cos I didn't know how to tell you if you were not a sweet spirit." The next day, when they met in the natural world in the campus, Benjamin asked her for another date. On that date he finally asked her to be his girlfriend and at once she said "yes."

Benjamin Strata had a light-complexion skin that looked like the white Caucasian skin of his fathers. He was just over 6 feet tall and weighed an average of 180 pounds. His forehead was flat and his chiseled face had grayish-blue eyes, black hair with tan strands, a well-shaped nose and thick brown lips. Benjamin had piercing eyes, a broad chest and flat abdomen.

Mr. Strata loved beautiful women with great voluptuous bodies. But he preferred those who had great curves and were from wealthy families. Perhaps his greatest skill was his ability to spot a business, venture or deal that had the potential to yield solid profits. His greatest ambition was to wield political power and control the lives of many people. Like his wife, he had no regard for religion or faith but he believed that to survive in life you must be spiritual.

Maraya Strata was a beautiful ebony-skinned woman. She stood at 5 feet 11 inches and was a big woman with a weight of about 180 pounds. She was tall and attractive with features that would make any man stop, stare and admire her for hours. Maraya had large size 36G breasts and a well-shaped figure '8' body with semi-wide hips. Her head was characterized by a pair of lovely brown eyes, short black hair, scanty eyebrows and a nose with a perfect shape. Both jaws were larger than normal and her lips were bright red. But she rarely showed her perfect white teeth whenever she smiled or spoke or laughed. Maraya hardly ever smiled but never wore a frown on her face. She walked in short steps and never forgot her sitting or standing manners.

Mrs. Maraya Strata was often reserved due to her ultra-conservative nature. Besides her beauty, she was brilliant, something which made her all the more desirable to men. She was spiritual but never dabbled into religion. Countless other men had tried to win her heart but there was only one man she loved, and his name was Benjamin Strata. She believed her greatest inheritance from her parents was her membership in the dark world. This was the one thing that had never failed to get her to wherever she desired to go and provide whatever she wished for in life. It was one part of her life that wasn't open to compromise.

Three months after they left university, Benjamin and Maraya had secured quality jobs. She had a job teaching molecular biology at the local community college while he worked with a multinational petroleum company as the manager of one of their oil refineries. They got married one year later after they had become financially stable. They bought a home in the affluent York region of Shiloh City and prepared to start a family. Ten months later they had their first child, and it was a boy. They called him 'Anino,' meaning, 'our firstborn' and they had four other children after him. Typical of families with such parents, all the children would have been initiated into the realm of power while still in the womb of their mother. As he entered his pre-school years, Maraya changed his name to Nino which meant 'first born.' She did this to indicate the importance she conferred on the fact that her first born son belonged to her.

Benjamin had vowed to be the best father he could for his family and was prepared for family life when his wife began having children. Nino, being the firstborn, had been born with many great expectations. Typical of the tradition of the people of the Stratas' tribe of *Itombi* of West-Central Cretania, the parents sought to know the destiny of their children as they were born. One day when baby Nino was twelve months old they took him to see a Calazari stargazer who lived on the outskirts of Shiloh. Pa Mateo, as the seer was fondly called, was about sixty years old and had been a stargazer for more than thirty years after learning the trade from his own father. The seer looked upon the child and rattled his tools. After asking the parents a few questions he began to beam with excitement. He clearly couldn't hide his feelings—just like a baby that had finally been rewarded with a rare toy he had requested from his parents but never got until now. And after a few minutes later when he seemed to have mellowed down, he took the baby from his mother and standing up raised the child to the heavens. A few moments passed as he spoke inaudible words. The he turned to the parents and he uttered his sayings. "Ha, ha, ha," the seer began by laughing and then continued.

"Finally the long wait is over and restoration begins. Benji, the God of gods has given you a great child and he will have a colorful life. But he will fight many battles because he will have many enemies. And that is because he will carry so much responsibility in his hands. His star will take down great stars but none will destroy him. Like a true lion, he will not succumb in battle. Your son will start from one side of the road and end on the other side. He will begin life riding a black horse but he will exchange it later in life for a white one. This is a true prince of *Itombi* and great leader of our people. A great star, a king of kings is what he is. That's all you need to know about him."

With those words he handed back the child to the parents and sat down not bothering to look at the faces of the perplexed parents. Nino's parents thanked Pa with the gifts they had brought for him and took their son and left. Maraya was happy at what she had heard because she felt it was a good prophecy. But Benjamin seemed a bit worried at what he heard. He thought to himself what it meant to "start life riding a black horse and exchange it for a white horse." "Surely it must mean sex or wives or marriages or something similar," Mr. Strata thought to himself. "He will marry a black woman first and then divorce her to marry a white one," Benjamin wondered. "Well as long as he is a powerful man he will be just fine," Benjamin muttered to his wife. "Yes, my dear. We have given him a great legacy to handle himself well in life," Maraya replied. They never talked about it ever again as they both agreed that their firstborn son had a good future.

When Nino turned three years old, his parents registered him in kindergarten and after two years he graduated and moved to primary school. He was not usually at the very top of his class but his grade point average was always within the 80th percentile in his class and in five years he finished primary school. He wrote and passed the secondary entrance examinations in Class 5 and his parents threw a small party on his behalf to show their joy and pride in their son. Due to his good grades he got accepted in one of the best private secondary school in the state of Shiloh, Saint Christopher's Secondary School. It was a mixed school with boys and girls in attendance. In the ninth month of that year Nino Strata began his secondary education. He was ten years old.

It was a Friday, three days before her first son would start secondary school and Maraya could not contain her joy. She had put him to bed every day for the past three weeks and read him his favorite stories and then kissed him to sleep. And on this day she did not expect the strange events that were about to unfold that night. As she retired to bed, she noticed something strange—her husband had gone to sleep before her. As trivial as it might seem, Maraya had come to understand that the most trivial of things usually had the greatest of consequences. Benjamin never went to sleep without her sleeping first. This had been a custom in this Strata household since the year the got married. A few minutes later, she waved it off as nothing and convinced herself it was no big deal. It had happened before and they were all still alive. At that point she asked herself why she was now associating life and death with the matter. As she mounted the bed, she stared at the face of her husband for a while and noticed yet another strange thing–Benjamin was snoring though not loud. "But

Benjamin never snored," she reminded herself. And then there was another uncommon occurrence, this time written on the wall of their bedroom. The digital clock on the wall was usually set to give the current time. But somehow, the clock had been advanced many years into the future to the time of the current month but a different day. "It must be Benjamin playing his usual time trivia and then forgot to change it back," she thought to herself. As she pondered all these things in her mind, she adjusted to her usual sleeping position on her bed and soon fell asleep.

The night was dark, and Maraya sat on one of the chairs in what looked like a theater. A little while later the show began. The first thing she noticed was a little square garden appearing in the middle of the stage. Soon after, a giant hand came down and set a small flower in the middle of the garden. The flower was beautiful indeed, and it had a pleasant fragrance, a pretty color and a pleasant look. And this flower flourished and grew and spread its petals around it. Then bees came and pollinated it and it produced seeds and its seeds were scattered all over the garden. Some fell into the good soil and germinated and produced great flowers themselves. Soon the whole garden had beautiful flowers with some having the same color as the parent flower and others having two colors. Other flowers had even more colors than those with two colors. And they were all beautiful to look at and each had a pleasant smell.

But not long after the beautiful flowers began to multiply and to fill the whole garden, another hand, dark and withered, came up from the ground and released seeds into the same garden. And at first, the dark seeds showed no life but after a while they entered into the good soil like the beautiful flowers and they grew and flourished. They grew so well that the evil plants produced by the dark seeds competed with, and overpowered, the beautiful flowers. The bad plants soon grew thorns and began to choke and destroy the beautiful flowers. This continued until Maraya looked and saw that all the beautiful flowers inside the garden had begun to wither away because of the wickedness of the dark and evil flowers.

As the battle continued between the good and bad plants and their seeds, the hand which was strong and pleasant to look at came down as it previously did. And the hand took three of the young ones of the beautiful flowers and transformed them into weapons and placed them in strong bags and laid them at her feet. The first weapon was a sword, the second one a bow and arrow and the third one was a fire princess. After this, the great hand left the stage and then there was a voice from above. It said, "Maraya, take these and nurture them and when they have grown, they will deliver the good and beautiful flowers in the great garden." As she gazed upon the sword, she discovered it had her name written on one half of the sword, together with the seal of her family line. Then Maraya tried to rise from her seat to take the three bags and nurture them as she had been commanded. But as much as Maraya tried, she realized that she could not nurture them. And it was because she was of the stock of the dark flowers and her hands were soiled with blood just like the evil flowers. Then the great voice came back to Maraya and spoke to her once again. It said, "You must take one side, great woman. Or isn't it your course to nurture these weapons until the appointed time and to be the cow that gives them milk?" These words spoken by the great voice terrified and confused her because she did not understand their meaning. Sensing her failure, she sought a place to hide herself from the great voice but found none. But her gestures suggested she wished she was on the side of the beautiful flower; because she purposed to wield the weapons and nurture them. Maraya hesitated on her decision until the evil dark hand took notice. At once, the evil hand rushed at her with a sword and plunged it into her heart and she died.

Not long after the great voice finished speaking, the evil hand once again came out of the ground. Having noticed what the great and mighty hand had done, it went to the garden. It gave power and wisdom to the dark plants to destroy the pleasant flowers and own the garden. The dark flowers troubled the beautiful flowers to destroy their beauty and kill their great fragrance. And then there was a union of dark flowers who had power to produce a great evil one, a dark flower more powerful than all the others. This evil flower became the leader of the dark flowers. And having so much power, this great dark flower rose to power over all in the garden. And she set out to destroy the beautiful flowers especially the special ones that shone like great stars.

Together, the evil hand and this great evil flower did great evil and destroyed many good flowers and many special flowers. And so, all the good garden flowers were in awe and terror of these great ones. And this greatest evil plant sought to destroy the whole garden itself so that the great garden would not strengthen any other garden on the stage. As she continued to look, Maraya saw the evil great one pursue the three weapons to destroy them from the garden and from the stage of the theater. And as they pursued the three, the great hand fought against them and they wounded the fiery weapon and destroyed many flowers that gave help to the weapons. But the three weapons survived alive. As she continued to look at the stage, the one that strengthened the sword had taken her place and had strengthened all the weapons bringing them together as one unit. On the day the weapons gathered under the great sun, they destroyed the great thorny plants. That was the day the great evil thorny flower died.

The next morning Maraya couldn't leave the bed when she woke up. She was feeling ill as she pondered the meaning of all the things she had seen. By the time she awoke, Benjamin had left for work and she heaved a sigh of relief. She cried as she usually did whenever she was so upset at something. She decided not to talk about the matter with Benjamin as he would be quite upset. He would accuse her of hallucinating or having dangerous illusions. He would drag her to the psychiatrist or some other mind doctor. She had seen her death, and her fear was justifiable. Though she knew what she had seen couldn't be a trivial matter she had no one to talk to about it. It was then she thought about her mother Mary-Ann and how she would consider the matter. But her mother was an old woman close to her eighties who was better left alone to age and die peacefully. Mary-Ann Nestel need not be bothered with such matters as dreams. And besides, her mother was never the dream-interpreting type. But Maraya knew what she had seen had something to do with her life and perhaps her future. And she had to find out its meaning somehow.

Sunday came too quickly but it was just two days after the events of the previous Friday. Maraya had been brooding over her experience like a chicken beaten by a rainstorm. She had avoided Benjamin all day on Saturday and had taken an excuse to go shopping early that Sunday. This way her husband would not try to spend time with her and notice that her attitude wasn't normal. "And for what?" she thought. "All because of one silly dream which was just a nightmare that can't be understood because of ignorance of such complex spiritual matters." As night approached, Maraya found herself much too unstable to read to Nino or put him to bed. So she delegated that task to the maid. And to her great relief, Mr. Strata had delayed in coming home probably out drinking with friends and co-workers. At about 11 p.m., she retired to bed after the usual night time tradition of watching the international news on cable television at 10 p.m. As she hit the sheets, she quickly fell asleep. And this sleep was deep because she didn't notice when her husband came back home or came into the room. It was the first time it had ever happened or first time in a long time.

Maraya walked hurriedly to the closest and safest space she could occupy in the middle of the railway tracks. It was not as dark as the other night but it was getting there fast. And the skies were a mix of blue and reddish-orange as dusk seemed to be approaching with furious speed. As she looked, there was a voice screaming for everyone, and anyone, to come and watch the great drama about to unfold. But as loud as the call was, there was no one else but Maraya herself watching the show. But then she noticed that many people were gathering on the side of the railway to her right. And all these people were dressed in white and had a pleasant aura, of brilliant white light, about them as though they were from the angelic realm. At a certain time there was a call to begin what she thought was a drama show about to take place. But much to her amazement there was a locomotive train that was coming up the tracks and headed for the light towards the end of the tracks. The train eventually entered into the light and then the tracks disappeared into the light. As the train approached, the people on the other side boarded in a hurry as though they were operating a timed schedule and were running out of time. Maraya immediately thought these angelic beings were trying to get back to heaven where they came from and so the train was coming to take them. To board the train which had now stopped on the tracks, the people had to walk on a paved walkway to get to the front of the train to access the train's entrance. But as the people dressed in white proceeded to board the train looking so joyful, people began to appear on the other side, the left side, of the rail tracks. And these looked dark and scruffy, dirty and evil. They had dark spikes coming out of their vests on their shoulders and the surrounding aura was a dark forbidden smoke like those of evil spirits. And as soon as they arrived, the dark ones began to throw great rocks at the good people to stop them from entering the train. At first the evil ones were failing but as the day got darker, they were getting more accurate because they were stronger in darkness than in light. And then a strange man came from the behind the good people and placed robes on three of the good people to empower them to destroy the evil people. And the good people called to Maraya to come and help them fight since she knew the enemies, how they came and how to stop them. But she realized that her bond to the left side was stronger than her ties to the good people. Maraya's hesitation made her an enemy to both sides. And in time another helper was chosen to strengthen the chosen ones of the good people. As the battle progressed, the evil people cast stones against the good ones and because they mistook Maraya for one of the good people they stoned her and she fell down on the tracks lifeless. And at the end of a great battle and many casualties, the chosen good ones overcame the strongest of the evil ones, and boarded the train, leaving the dark ones in the dark world.

As she woke up this time, she found she wasn't crying though a few tears rolled down her cheeks. She noticed it was reading about 5 a.m. on the clock and Benjamin was still asleep but wasn't snoring this time. Somehow she felt a little comfort because of that absence of deep emotions. She felt so much joy because now she knew for sure that this was the future revealed to her and that the good people won at last. But she wasn't sure if she was one of the good people or one of the bad ones. And she was even more confused because she wasn't sure what it all really meant. Later that morning, when they were at the breakfast table at 7:10 a.m., she finally found the courage to ask her husband the biggest question troubling her mind.

"Benjamin dearest, I have a question to ask you and I need you to be straight and truthful with me. Okay, my darling?" She asked her husband. "Maraya, I am always honest with you so go ahead and ask," Mr. Strata replied. "Am I a good or bad person in your most brutal and honest of judgments?" Maraya asked her husband.

He was surprised at first but thought it was the beginning of one of her humorous conversations. "You are normally a good person who can be bad sometimes. And I mean that very much," Benjamin replied. And much to his surprise, she asked no other questions. Two minutes later, she kissed him to thank him as was her custom. Then she got up from the table and headed out the door to drop Nino off for his first day at school before she went to work. As the car pulled up to the gates of Saint Christopher's, she held her son's hands and kissed his forehead to reassure him again that everything would be okay. And as she kissed him she hoped deep down in her mind that her dreams were not predicting a bad omen for her son. And then she took him inside the school to register him.

CHAPTER TWO

Sowing the Seeds of Light amidst the Darkness

Nino's journey through the five years of secondary school passed by in a hurry and was mostly without incident. The exceptions were in the second and fourth years when he had an infectious disease and a mysterious illness respectively. Then in the final year at Saint Christopher's, a couple of incidents occurred during the final semester of that year. The first one was on the day of the release of the results of the final school examinations. It was a warm and humid afternoon when the two young ladies from Class 5 Beta passed through Nino's class, Class 5 Gamma, but didn't find him there. They kept searching until they finally found and interrupted him. He was near the school gate and on his way home after school. Mimi Pockets and Vivian Brown had joined the school's Christian Student Fellowship since they were in their first year in school. Mimi joined during the first school day and Vivian did same during the second semester. Mimi's father was the senior pastor of a medium-sized church located in the religious district of Shiloh called Mount Zion; while Vivian attended a small church outside of Mount Zion. On this day, both ladies had planned as part of their team evangelism drive to talk to four of their colleagues that week. One of them was Nino Strata who was famous in school for his staunch opposition to religion and Christianity in particular. He hated the students in the CSF as they were popularly called. It was no secret that Nino was one of the most evil of all the students in the school as he was rumored to be one of the heads of the local school coven. He had the reputation for using his spiritual and financial influences to achieve whatever he wanted. These desires included ladies both inside and outside of school whether they were within his age-group or were older than he was.

But the Christian students who were members of the CSF had a reputation for their fearlessness. They had approached all the boys and girls in the school regardless of their fearsome reputations. They had also spoken to every teacher and staff in the school about their faith damning the consequences of their action. And on this day the Christian students would make Nino hear what their Lord, Jesus, had to say to him. Vivian had informed him that she and Mimi were coming to have a talk with him and he immediately knew what it was about. Mimi Pockets was one of the relentless evangelists in school while Vivian Brown was known for her powerful anointed prayers.

"Hello Nino, how do you today?" were the words from Mimi who spoke first as Vivian offered an enthusiastic wave of the hand. "Hello ladies, Mimi and Vivian. I'm OK I guess," replied Nino. "We won't take much of your time, Nino just a little talk about Jesus," said Mimi. "Nino, do you realize that Jesus loves you and has saved your life from death not once but many times." "How do you mean, Mimi?" Nino replied. "Well, I know that Jesus died to save you from your sins, he saved you when you almost died three years ago of the pox and again that night in Class 4 last year when you were bleeding uncontrollably from your nose."

"Why do you say so," Nino replied angrily and surprised. It was then Vivian cut in. "Nino, what Mimi is trying to say is this—each time you had your health problems and had to be admitted in the clinic, both of us and other CSF members prayed all night for you until your health recovered." Nino was so dumbfounded at what he was hearing he asked, "Can you prove this?" Vivian answered at once, "Yes we can, Nino. Remember when you had the pox, you met a nurse in your dream that treated you and told you that you will recover in three days and you did?" Vivian paused for a second and then resumed speaking. "And remember when you were bleeding, you used a handkerchief which was from one of our CSF colleagues to apply on your nose and then it immediately stopped?" Now, Nino was terrified at Vivian's words.

"But why did you wait all this time to tell me this?" he stuttered. Mimi replied, "The Lord speaks at the appointed time, Nino, and that time is now for you to come to Jesus and make him your Lord and Savior." Mimi paused for a while before resuming. "There is a special calling on your life Nino. You have a great star and if you are not careful with your life it may be destroyed even before the time. And then that great destiny would be gone and useless." Nino looked hard at the ceiling for a few minutes and then turned to the ladies and told them he would think about it for a few days before responding. "OK then," Vivian replied. "Please let us know whenever you're ready. God bless you, Mr. Strata." And with those final words from Vivian, the ladies both left him. Mimi's words kept on echoing in his head — "There is a special calling on your life." "But what could this 'calling' be?" he wondered aloud. Nino swore as he rode back home in the black chauffeured Mercedes Benz S Class limousine that took him to and from school every day. He swore he would never become a Christian regardless of what the ladies said about his destiny and being cautious so that he doesn't destroy his life. But deep within his heart, he was a little worried about the incident. He was Nino Strata, a young man from a family of wealth and power and no amount of Christian preaching would terrify him. Nino Strata would see neither Mimi nor Vivian again throughout secondary school.

But Mimi Pockets was the most beautiful girl in the whole school and Nino was hiding the strong feelings he had for her. He dared not try to date her as failure could earn him a bad reputation. But it would also condemn him to a semester or more of harassment, and perhaps beatings, by those boys who had a crush on her and had warned other boys to stay away from her. Most of the strongest, roughest and richest boys in the school had tried to date Mimi. But none of them had ever succeeded even though they had tried many times. Nino knew it was pointless trying to date Mimi Pockets because not only was she pretty she came from a family with deep pockets and great spiritual power. Everyone knew that the Pockets family were wealthy as they owned businesses and shares of companies located all over the world. They were also great Christians who took their faith seriously. And many members of the Pockets family had citizenships of countries beside Cretania. For instance, Bishop Pockets who was the bishop of Mount Zion Pentecostal and Mimi's father had the passports of three different countries including Cretania. These nations included the United States of America, Great Britain, and the Cayman Islands. And, of course, they were Cretanians. This made Mimi a citizen of all these countries and much sought-after as a girlfriend or wife. In Cretania, holding passports from other countries wasn't much of a great achievement because Cretania was wealthy and highly successful. But having citizenship from a country equal, or greater, in economic or development status, increased your own status in the society. But the primary reason Mimi Pockets was so much in demand was that she was also a virgin. And she was a young, brilliant and beautiful virgin for that matter. And because of all these reasons she was one of the most prestigious and sought-after spinsters in Cretania.

The second incident occurred not long after Nino's talk with Mimi and her friend. Three months after talking with the ladies, most final year students gathered at the principal's office to pick up their results in the final secondary school examination. As the students received their results some of them burst into shouts of joy and laughter while others became silent and left the school in a hurry. Nino passed with 3 alphas and 5 betas and he was overwhelmed with joy. He made his A's in Mathematics, English and Chemistry as he expected, and scored B's in Physics, Biology and all his other subjects. Those who passed headed for the local bar and restaurant outside the school premises called 'Cooley's Bar.' Every student in the school was familiar with the joint and frequented it often. Its owner and operator was Ma Cooley, the 65 year old former principal of one of the competing secondary schools in the area called Shiloh Collegiate High School. The bar had both good and nefarious reputations. Many considered it good because it had excellent food and cuisine and drinks with great staff well-versed in nutrition and food preparation. But, it had a dark side to it as it was a well-known fact that the thick plantation behind the restaurant was a meeting place for all the witches and wizards who were students in the school and those from the other schools in the community.

As the souls of the students left their bodies and gathered in the plantation, the time had just clocked 11 a.m. Nino arrived at the same time as his new girlfriend Belinda Satchi. Unknown to him, she had also been dating another student, a boy named Alfred Kayto who was hoping to marry her someday. As Nino and Belinda met, they embraced warmly and Alfred saw this as it happened. He couldn't contain his envy and confronted Nino at once with a 20-inch metal rod in his hand. "Nino,

Belinda is my girlfriend so you better leave her alone and find your own lady," Alfred shouted at Nino threatening him with the rod in his hand. "We are supposed to be brothers and you dare threaten me. I am the leader in this place and don't you ever forget that," Nino replied. Alfred shouted back at Nino, "I love my woman more than this useless coven if that's what you mean, and that means you are not my brother at all."

"If you don't let her go right now, you worthless mulatto, I will use this pipe to smash your miserable head, Nino," Alfred shouted back at Nino. "I am not your girlfriend, Alfred. We are just good friends," Belinda shouted to interrupt the heated exchange. Nino felt insulted by Alfred's words and wanted to humiliate him in front of everyone especially Belinda. He drew Belinda towards him and kissed her passionately on her lips. This infuriated Alfred who ran towards him and attacked him furiously with the metal rod. Nino quickly pushed Belinda aside and stepped aside to avoid the blow of the rod. The teenage Mr. Strata had a brown belt in Karate and had the fighting skills he could employ to protect himself and

Belinda. Nino kicked the rod out of Alfred's hand and grasped his opponent's head in a tight grip. Alfred replied with punches to the chest of Nino and they fought for a few seconds exchanging blows and kicks. At last, Nino had Alfred on the floor and sat on him in a submission hold. Other students had come to separate the fight and as Alfred got to his feet he vowed he would get his revenge. "I will find you someday Nino and kill you even though we have left school, and you can keep that whore 'cos I never wanted her anyway," Alfred screamed at Nino. "And let me tell you something Nino, I know all your secrets—every last one of them. Last semester when Ninita died I know she died because of you. You and your friends killed her using your powers. Well, let me tell you something, fool, from where I come from, this power is for little boys like you. And this is all you have but to me it is nothing. What we have is by far stronger than this and one day you will understand what I mean." Nino was stunned by the accusation and the many sighs from the people around made him all the more intimidated.

Kayto continued speaking with his voice raised even more. "We celebrate our birthdays on the moon and we drink nothing but strong red and eat fresh young chicks, all virgins, just let me tell you. Don't even try me, or else. I see you are all little boys and girls in this school and none of you will ever reach my level with power. I swear you will see what I will do to some of you in this school, just watch me. As for you Nino the bastard or whatever you call yourself, this is what I will do to you–I will take your own cow from you and I will milk her day and night anywhere, anyhow and anytime I want. And when I finish I will then use her to gore your life out of you. I swear I will do it and you will all see."

There was a thunderous applause from some of the others in that dark place. Shouts of "Teach him a lesson Ani," "Nino, you must give him your reply now," and "Kill Alfred now, he is a true bastard" rented the air. But Nino did nothing and most importantly said nothing.

Nino and Belinda returned to their bodies in the restaurant and went to their respective homes without talking about what happened in the coven.

Alfred was not physically near the restaurant and the two lovers thought little about what had happened. And when Nino got home, he narrated the story to his mother privately. But unknown to him, he had made a great enemy for life in Alfred Kayto.

****

On the next Saturday of the next weekend after the confrontation with Kayto, Nino and Belinda had agreed to meet for a date at some low-key bar not far from his home. This was for two reasons, the first being that if her parents caught them at the bar they could come up with the excuse that they were meeting some classmates for finals celebration. And second, if they needed a more private place they could go to his home when his parents were at work for the day. On that Saturday, Nino arrived first as he had been taught by his parents — "Always arrive at least half an hour early because you never know what good things may be waiting before others arrive." Belinda arrived forty minutes later complaining of the traffic. They immediately ran into each other with a warm embrace and then sat down. He did the orderings and both of them each had a jug of chilled Heineken beer with salted cashew nuts. Belinda had come prepared with questions to ask Nino about some of the issues raised by Kayto in the week that had just passed. And in particular was the issue of the death of Ninita Thorn. She was allegedly killed by one of her boyfriends on the order of someone quite influential in her family. Ninita was pretty and had a great body and it was believed she had many boyfriends with many of them much older than her. And one of her many boyfriends was Nino Strata — her youngest, and only, secondary school lover. Rumor had it that she was the richest in the family due to the number of sugar daddies she had, something that made her many enemies both within and without her family. There were few stories of how she died but the list of the potential suspects was endless. At the top of the list was her father, Velosos Thorn. Mr. Thorn was so poor, working a warehouse manager job, he often had to borrow just to pay his bills and feed himself and his family. He was reportedly worth about 50,000 cretari before Ninita's death. But in the few days after the tragic event, his net worth grew to 20 million cretari. It was a suspicious development indeed. And the strangest of all was that he went on a shopping spree which included buying buses for the school she attended in honor of her memory. Besides, it wasn't a hidden secret that Mr. Thorn was a member of the one of the darkest, most feared and most evil secret societies in Cretania. It was called *The Society* and its members were some of the most dreaded members of Cretanian society. Those members were popularly called *Societarians* by everyone. The most feared of all the secret societies was the very powerful and extremely mysterious *Pentosi*—the group of the five most powerful men and evil spirits in Cretania. Any public mention of the names of these groups was totally forbidden in the country.

And the next on the list was Ninita's stepmother, Dede, who was rumored to have married Velosos just to secure her job at the warehouse clearing company in which she worked. Dede worked as Mr. Thorn's secretary. Before Ninita's death, Dede lived from paycheck to paycheck and was just barely surviving her hard knock life. But she was now worth a whopping 3 million cretari. And there was also the aunt, Kiki, Velosos' younger and only sibling, who worked as a lowly bank clerk but now had a net worth of 1 million cretari. Most people suspected that it was one or more of them who organized Ninita's cold-blooded sacrifice for the sake of getting great riches overnight. People in the extended family knew they were all guilty of the crime.

Belinda had also heard the rumors that her current lover Nino was in on the whole thing. But his saving grace of an alibi was that he was no richer after the incident because if he was everyone would have made him the primary suspect. Everyone would know of his new-found wealth. His father Benjamin kept an eye on the bank account and assets of all his children and if any of them had suddenly acquired riches, he would have sent that child out of the house to survive on his or her own. Still, she knew she had to ask him because the last thing she wanted was to be in love with a murderer. And besides, if it was true that Nino was guilty, she herself could well be the next Ninita. There were too many things running through

Belinda's mind. Many of her friends and advisers including her parents who knew about the relationship warned her to be cautious so as not to be the next dead girlfriend of the popular, handsome and charismatic Nino Strata. So she made up her mind on what to do. She had gone with one of her friends to the most powerful male *tatu*, a witch doctor, in the city. And the *tatu* had given her a white powdery substance which he called "local truth serum."

"Put a little bit of this in his drink and he will tell you all that you need to know — the truth, the whole truth and nothing but the truth." Belinda believed him and took the white nylon bag containing the stuff, paid for it and left with her friend. As soon as she noticed Nino was glued to the TV screen, she made her move. As she pretended to place her bag on her laps she grabbed some of the white powder between her right thumb and index finger. Then she moved her left hand as if to play with his hair by smoothening it. As she did this, she released the powdery substance into his drink as he smiled at her with his usual babyish look on his face. She then withdrew both hands and watched as the powder spontaneously dissolved as it entered his drink. As if on cue, he picked up the glass of beer and took three big gulps and put the glass back on the table. She watched him and waited for about a minute while hoping her scheme had worked.

Finally she spoke as he turned from the TV screen to gaze upon her beauty. "Nino, did you silence Ninita? And was she really your girlfriend or was it just a play-play thing?" Nino was stuck by the question and immediately lost his voice. He was silent for about three minutes while Belinda poured some of her beer into his glass to top it up; and then offered to give him to drink from her glass, praying on the inside he would notice nothing. Eventually, Nino spoke stuttering. "Me, no way it could have been me. I would love to tell you if I knew but I swear it, Bel, I don't know if it was me. Believe me, I assure you of that. It was like a dream—it was all a blur. If it was me I can't remember and I mean that so much."

Belinda was dumbfounded at this seeming confession. "How could Nino not be sure if it was him or someone else?" she thought to herself. This was all she needed for a confession. Most of her friends and her mother were right. "Nino had something to do with Ninita's death and perhaps was either solely or primarily responsible for that poor girl's death," she wondered in her mind. But Belinda wanted to hear more so she leaned gently towards him and kissed him on his forehead while trying to hide her emotions at the same time.

"Did you fly to her place that night and was she there?" Belinda asked in a hushed tone. "Yes," he replied, "And no. It is all so confusing now in hindsight." "So what do you think happened?" Belinda quizzed him further. "I believe it was all evil powers at work, you know those very dark terrible powers," Nino replied. Belinda smiled as if to say "OK, I believe you so just forget about it."

But then Nino continued. "Belinda I need to tell you a secret you must forever keep, please. Do you promise?" "OK," Belinda replied. "Thank God the truth powder is working." She thought to herself.

"Something strange happened last semester between her father, herself, me and others. Ninita confided in me many times that she felt unsafe with her family, like they were trying to harm her or something. So one day on the awards ceremony night, her father comes driving a black hearse van with a black mini coffin inside the back side of the van. I thought nothing of it at the time but now it scares me. Nini and I were together and he found us near the cafeteria area. She didn't hug him or even kiss him. She just said "Hi, dad" and that was all. She introduced me as her friend from the same class and I shook his hand but he didn't seem interested in that so I withdrew my hands. He seemed upset at something and soon enough I found out. After Ninita excused herself to go and get something to drink, her stepmother joined us. She began to ask me if I wanted a job that will pay me more than I could ever imagine. Of course I said yes but more out of curiosity than anything else. She laughed saying there was no one in my shoes who would not want such a job. About that time, Mr. Velosos gave her a curious look and she stopped speaking to me at once. He then asked me if I was his daughter's boyfriend and that if I was he would want us to be closer together. I said I was her boyfriend for sure and I would love to talk to Ninita about the job first before accepting it if I chose to do so. It was at this point I began to realize that they were not a close-knit family at all. About this time Ninita came back with our drinks and didn't even look at any one of them. She had a worried look on her face that I couldn't quite understand. As she placed the tray of drinks on the table nearest us, she grabbed my right hand and led me out of there fast. It was all so strange and curious."

"Can you tell me how he looks—you know, the monster?" Belinda asked. "Of course, I can. He wore a blue caftan and you could tell from his accent he was from the West Indies originally. His eyes were cold as hell and he had a stare like he was about to go and murder someone a.s.a.p., you know. He was quite tall—about 5-11 to 6 feet tall with a light-reddish complexion. He had chiseled facial attributes—his nose looked like it was chiseled out of wood and attached to his face. His jaw bones were visible on both sides and there was hardly any flesh on it. And his cheek bones were not only visible but they could be seen forming a distinguishing contour on his face below his eyes. Those evil eyes were gray in color just like Ninita's.

He looked like he was starving to death but Ninita informed me that his slim build was his natural stature. He married Ninita's mother back in the West Indies and they produced her with mixed race attributes as expected because her mother, Tina, is black. But she left him once they got to this country so she could return to their country. But he tricked her into leaving behind Ninita, who was just a little child at the time. Neither mother nor daughter has forgiven him for that ever since then. That was about twelve to thirteen years ago and Nini loved it here cos of all the rich guys who dated her and made her rich. But her mother had pleaded for her to return with all the money she had made and saved up but she refused. Ninita was very greedy when it came to money—she wanted more and more and more. She had to live the good life, the hi-life. And it was too much of that good life which eventually killed her. And besides that she was quite successful at what she did so she had many enemies just because of that success."

"I hear she only agreed to become your girlfriend cos your parents are loaded," Belinda teased him. "Of course, and she never tried to hide the fact that she was a high-class super-expensive whore. I fell for her beauty and that gorgeous, drop-dead body. Do you know they called her the 'Picasso' of the escort business? She was, simply put, a genius of the whore business. The way she charmed her clients, how she seduced those who were not willing to give in to her demands whatever they were, the sheer beauty of her pose, the elegance of her gait and, of course, her riches. Gosh, she was the best at what she did, Bel, for real. But that by itself wasn't what made her so many enemies. A few big politicians and businessmen in this state and in the country had been conquered in her bed. And it was the combination of all that power and riches at her young age that made her so many enemies. But it was her sheer naivety that killed her. Oh my sweet, beautiful, foolish Nini—she has gone and left me all alone."

"Did you have sex with her stepmother, Dede? There's a rumor that you were also having an affair with her." "Maybe I did, Belinda. Dede and I had sex many times whenever Nini and her father were not around. She wanted me to do something secret and evil for her but I never guessed it was to kill Ninita. She seduced me with her beauty cos I never wanted to date her in the first place. Those ladies were crazy, you know. If they like a guy they give him anything he wants at any time. Please keep this secret or her father will kill me if it gets out."

"I hope they find all the guilty ones, Nino — at least for your sakes and all the other men who were dating her." "If I ever lay my hands on political power or serious money I will kill them all — the suspects, that is — by having them executed and publicly too. I swear it, Belinda, I loved her so much. And she loved me too. Remember, Belinda, all this must be strictly between us both only. If my family, especially my father, finds out, I am finished. And that's for real pretty one, for real." Nino had spoken his last words in the conversation.

"I promise Ani, it's just me and you forever, I swear it." Belinda moved closer to Nino once again and this time planted a kiss on his lips. Belinda had made up her mind about the relationship but she hid her feelings from him. She knew she would never see him again. A few minutes later they both left the bar holding hands as they usually did in public.

CHAPTER THREE

Transition to the Real World

Nino Strata was so popular in secondary school that he had many enemies especially the boys in his set and those in senior classes. He believed it was the combination of his good looks, athleticism and his family's wealth. But his friends flattered him that it was because many female students were trying to meet and date him. As he entered into university, he hoped to keep a low profile throughout his schooling and avoid such popularity in university. He had gained admission into the alma mater of his parents, the University of Shiloh, Shiloh City, to study chemical engineering just like his father. Just like his father, he met his future wife Mona Lee Spitzum in his first year. They met in one of the classes in the medical school where Mona was studying to get a 2-year pre-medical degree. Then she would enter the 4-year medical degree program. She was desperate to earn the Doctor of Medicine, M.D., degree. Nino was there to see one of his roommates and it was by chance they met. They began dating after a few weeks of repeated attempts by Nino to date Mona who refused at first but later agreed just to try him out. By their third year, they were two years into the relationship and talk of marriage had been brought up a few times by Mr. Strata. By their fourth year, they had verbally agreed to get married after they finished school when he would have his doctorate degree in chemical engineering and she would be an M.D. They both met each other's parents and their parents gave their consent to the relationship and the future marriage. Nino and Mona both spent six years in the university after which they earned their degrees. They then left school to embark on the next stage in their respective careers. She began her residency in surgery and he began work in the biggest Oil and Gas Sales and Distribution Company in Cretania. She began work after her residency as a General Surgeon at Shiloh General Hospital. He was working as a senior laboratory scientist with SOG, the Shiloh Oil & Gas Company.

****

At adulthood, Nino was exactly six feet tall and weighed about 190 to 200 pounds. He inherited his father's light skin complexion, broad chest, muscular build and love for cool and expensive toys. He had a chiseled nose, brown eyes, black hair and large mandibles which he got from his mother. His mother taught him to always try to put a smile on his face often and he had dark-brown lips which he often pursed. When he smiled or laughed, Nino exposed thirty-two teeth which were sparkling white. He had six-pack abs, and he often stared at people with a sharp and focused gaze.

Anino Strata had grown up to be a proud man just like his parents. He had inherited a love of flashy and expensive things—Rolex and Cartier watches, Maybach and Porsche cars, and of course, his father's Gulfstream G200 airplane. He was born into middle-class riches and over the years those riches had grown to become great wealth and Nino loved that life very much. The trips to great foreign cities, the flights on daddy's private jet around the world and the royalty treatment they got everywhere they went were some of the best times of his life. The combination of his father's conservative-liberal ideals and Maraya's ultra-conservative nature had been inculcated into him and had become part of his nature.

Just like Benjamin, his father, Nino Strata had an insatiable appetite for beautiful women with great anatomies. He had no preference for any skin complexion as long as the woman was pretty and attractive, had great personality and liked him very much. His goal in life was to be a great engineer and perhaps surpass his father's reputation in this area. He was not much of a believer in destiny because, just like his parents, he was not religious although he was quite spiritual like they were. At this age, he owned an expensive wardrobe, gadgets and machines. He had a Porsche Cayenne Turbo, Mercedes-Benz C-Class, Maybach 57 and Hummer H2. Every five years he bought a new Rolex watch and he had every new mobile phone with a major improvement.

Dr. Nino Strata and Dr. Mona Spitzum got married about twelve months after they both graduated from university. He was 23 years, and she was 22 years old when they got married. At first in the first few years of the marriage, everything worked perfectly and married life went smoothly. Then five years went by and Mona hadn't become pregnant and the Strata family began asking questions. Nino intervened in the attack on his wife by his family. He then insisted that she set up an appointment with her gynecologist friends to perform tests to discover what was wrong. They eventually saw one of her colleagues, Dr. Stella Sharp, who was a consultant 'OBGYN' with SGH. After performing the tests, they were both relieved as Dr. Sharp had informed them there seemed to be nothing wrong with Mona. When the tests returned, the gynecologist was proven right. There was nothing abnormal with the reproductive system of Dr. Mona Strata. The couple then decided they should be patient and wait for another few years to have children. But in those years they were waiting for Mona to get pregnant, a series of problems arose in the Strata family.

Nino got a call on his phone by his father one warm evening because something important had happened in his parents' home. When he got there, he found two medical doctors in the living room and an ambulance in the driveway. His siblings were all there and they all seemed to be mourning someone. He immediately noticed his mother was not there which was quite strange as she was always visible when people came over to visit. His father called him aside and broke the news about Maraya. Nino sighed out loud as he placed his hands over his head. He sank into her favorite leather chair and began sobbing. He couldn't think of anything but how she kept telling him they had important things to discuss with him. She would always postpone and tease him while telling him to take good care of himself, his wife and family. There was something on her mind but he could never figure it out. And now she was gone just like that without any goodbyes. His siblings came over to where he sat and they all consoled one another.

Maraya had passed away from what seemed to be a genetic heart problem which she inherited from one of her parents. It was then the family understood why their mother and wife had two mild heart attacks in her late forties and early fifties. And she seemed to have had a full recovery. Or so they thought. But her death had come suddenly and without warning. Due to the ignorance of her doctors to her condition she suffered terribly. As everyone thought she had recovered, tragedy struck. Suddenly, there was a sharp deterioration in the ability of the heart electrical trigger mechanism. The primary sites in the heart responsible for the generation of electrical impulses had suddenly ceased functioning. This primary site, the Sino-Atrial node, had ceased generating electrical impulses needed to stimulate the heart into beating and sending oxygenated blood from the lungs to the rest of the body. It was the same disease that struck the secondary site, the Atrio-Ventricular node. Because of this, the heart rate had slowed to less than twelve beats per minute. What followed was a generalized ischemia and death of tissues and cells due to hypoxia and oxygen deprivation to the body. She was dead even before people around her knew what she was suffering.

Maraya Strata was barely in her mid-sixties. The family doctors were not sure what it was but they believed it was a congenital heart disease. They didn't know its specific name and neither did the cardiac specialists. But the doctors wanted all the Strata children to undergo a battery of tests that could reveal just what the problem was. And the tests could also reveal the presence of the same condition in each one of them. Nino and all his siblings including their respective children all took the medical tests. The tests showed that the illness was a hereditary genetic condition. When the results came back it was discovered that two of Maraya's children had the condition and Nino was one of them.

As the family was still mourning Maraya's death, another problem reared its head this time in the household of Nino and his wife. A few months after the discovery of the genetic condition in the family, the stress and constant worrying seemed to be taking a toll on all the members of the family. Benjamin had been hospitalized once for what he insisted was heat stroke but his children knew better; because he had never had that condition before not to mention being admitted for it. Both of Nino's immediate siblings had quit their jobs to study genetics and this newly discovered family condition in particular. As for Nino, the news had taken a terrible toll on him.

A few months after Maraya's death, something strange happened in the Nino Strata home. One night Nino suddenly came to himself and realized he was standing on the rooftop of his family home. It was the loud scream of his wife that woke him up. Mona had woken up when she heard loud footsteps on the roof and discovered her husband was missing from their bed. She ran to the roof and found him there and yelled out his name at the top of her voice. Mona Strata quickly called the police and ambulance and her husband was taken to the hospital for examination. She knew at once what had happened—her husband had begun sleepwalking. Dr. Mona Strata considered the matter a very disturbing development in the family. Later that week, Nino confided in his wife that he had been having bad nightmares and that was maybe the cause of the problem. Mona booked appointments with the psychiatry department at SGH for Nino to see if that could help. But the couple had been drifting apart for a while since Mona's barrenness seemed obvious. The marriage was suffering from all the issues that had arisen in the family. Things would reach a climax a few months later one warm night in the first week of September.

It was a hard day at work and both Nino and Mona had returned late in the night. Because there was so much to do and Mona was too tired to do any house chores she instructed the housemaid, Lena, to work overtime for the night. About 5 a.m. in the morning, the scream of the housemaid had woken up Nino and the neighbors on either side of the Strata home. What she saw completely terrified her. Lena had heard the muffled screams of her mistress coming from the bedroom. She thought it was strange, so she decided to check out what was happening. As she knocked on the door, she discovered that the door was open. She then drew closer and found her mistress's blood-soaked body being choked to death by her husband. And a quick glance at Mona seemed to show that her body was lifeless in front of her husband who seemed to be asleep. She saw the bloody knife on the floor beside the bed by the side on which Mona had slept. Lena immediately remembered the rumors she had heard about Nino's sleepwalking and understood what was happening. The maid screamed at the top of her voice. As soon as she screamed Nino woke up and came to himself. A few seconds after, he fainted on the bed beside his wife when he saw what had happened to her and her current state. Lena called the police and an ambulance as she simultaneously tried to find out if Mona was still alive. She knew nothing about first-aid so she did not try to administer it to her boss but instead kept shouting her name hysterically. The ambulance came about seven minutes later and took Mona to the hospital while another ambulance had arrived to take Nino to a different hospital. Lena gave her statement to the police later. The news became front-page headlines in Shiloh the next day: "Oil Company Top Shot Strangles Wife to Death." In summary, the story said that an oil company top-shot had stabbed his wife five times in the chest while she was asleep and he claimed he was sleepwalking. And when the eyewitness came into the scene, he was not choking her but trying to wake her up once he realized what he had done. The police began their investigation after speaking to the eyewitness. They alerted the psychologists and psychoanalysts as they didn't know at first with what they were dealing. So they confined the top suspect, who had been identified as Dr. Nino Strata, in hospital as they conducted their investigations. The case against him was so strong because there was an eyewitness involved.

When news of what had happened to Nino reached Benjamin Strata he needed no one to tell him that there was a terrible misfortune working against his family. He had many suspects but didn't know which ones could be responsible. He knew he had many enemies both inside the family and many more outside of it. But who could have gotten so close to his family to inflict such damage? Benjamin took a mental look at himself and all he had achieved. He was a leader in the financial and business sector in the country and that alone was enough to make him many enemies in the country. But it was not only that he was one of the wealthiest men in Cretania, and often considered by people, at home and abroad, to be one of the most influential Cretanians. Benjamin Strata had become one of the wealthiest men in Cretania over the past thirty years. He was one of twenty known billionaires in the country and perhaps the wealthiest one from the state of Calazar. However, it was a well-known fact that there were at least forty billionaires in the country but most of them chose to be secretive about their wealth. But it was not the fact that Mr. Strata was wealthy today that scared and irked so many people. But it was the fact that his wealth was expected to grow considerably. This was because all his investments were still increasing in value and many were bringing in more income. For instance, his investments in gold and copper were not only in the raw commodities like bullion and reserves but also in stock of mining and utility companies. And the prices of commodities had been rising over the past two decades due to the boom in industrialization in the developing nations of the world. He also had the second largest gold reserve in the country second only to the State Treasury of Cretania which was the nation's central bank. Every other politician came to Benjamin Strata to borrow money for their election campaigns. And most people came to him via one of his companies to borrow money for their financial needs and capital for business ventures. It was only a matter of time before money power became political power.

Most people believed that for anyone to have all that wealth they had to be a member of the much-dreaded Pentosi. This was the society of five men who were overseen by the demon king who ruled the country from the second heavens. And after receiving authority and power from the king, these men determined everything that happened in the country. They influenced everything from politics to finance to business to development to education to pretty much everything. They determined who became president of the country and even most of the legislature, not to mention the judiciary. He knew that if the Pentosi had something to do with this, it was because someone in there saw him as a threat to holding the highest office in the land someday. It was the unspoken law in Cretania to eliminate all potential candidates for high office until only the chosen one is left. That way there will be no contender for the people to choose when time for election came. Mr. Strata knew that he was a strong contender for the office of president but he really had no intentions of running for that office. Maraya had pleaded with him that it was too dangerous for them and their family. And he knew that his wife couldn't have suddenly developed a genetic heart problem because they would have known all these years.

Besides, she was a strong woman who didn't give up easily without a great fight. Then there was the incident involving Nino, and his possible imprisonment for probably years or even decades. And it was all for a crime he knew his son didn't commit and was just being set up. It was all an attack from forces he couldn't see now but would soon find out. He knew the moment of truth his father always warned him about had finally come. Benjamin knew for certain he would be in the next federal government but didn't know in what capacity and how powerful his office would be. He suspected it would most probably be the office of Petroleum Industry, or even Science and Technology or maybe even Defense. He thought it wiser to wait till he got into office to seek and get revenge for his family. It was at this point he thought about his colleagues in The Society. He knew many of them would want to get rid of him so they could take his position and even his money. He knew at least one of them was involved but the only two names he could think of would not even dare. Not now when it was certain he would be in the next government with the election only a few months away.

And then Benjamin focussed on the inside of his family. His parents were dead so they couldn't possibly be behind it. And even if they were alive they loved him too much to harm him in any way. He was their first child and main hope to achieve greatness for the family name. But all his three siblings were still alive. The immediate junior siblings, who were twin girls, Sophie and Michaela, loved him too much to harm him. They would die for him and on many occasions they had each almost lost their lives just trying to fight to get him to where he was today. It was for that reason they were both chief executive officers of two of the largest corporations in Cretania; and why they were two of the wealthiest women in the world. His youngest sibling was John Joe Strata who was one of the smartest minds in the field of biotechnology in the country and the whole world. JJ Strata had no particular reason to hate him and his achievements. But Benjamin and JJ had seen their fair share of quarrels which he once attributed to sibling rivalry. But as they grew older, things between them grew sour as his younger brother accused him of neglecting his family responsibilities due to his wealth and popularity. Benjamin suspected that years of no communication between them may have caused his brother to finally give in to assisting his external enemies against him. But, of course, this was all just a wild thought because he still believed JJ loved him so much and would never try to hurt him and his family.

But Benjamin had decided he won't wait for the future to find out what was going on about him and his family. He remembered the old man who had been a seer to Maraya and her family for years. It was the same one who they had gone to when each of their children were born, to look into the star and future of that child. The same man had foretold the stars of Nino, Monaya and her twin sister Catherine, and their junior brothers, the twin boys Clement and Christoff. As he called the old seer's office to schedule an appointment, he discovered the old man was ill from old age but would see him on one condition and just for a few minutes. Benjamin knew what the condition was. There was only one thing an old man dying of old age wanted more than anything else. It had to be a large amount of assets to leave as inheritance to his children when he was gone. So he took two cartons filled with cash, and three boxes filled with brand new personal items like clothes and shoes. Then he added two large high definition TV sets and one large two door high-end Samsung refrigerator and a deep freezer. He loaded all these items into a large truck after hiring three workers to load and unload the truck and another one to drive the truck.

As he drove to the village where the seer lived, the truck followed closely behind him. As they arrived, it seemed the whole household was there just waiting to receive him. It was a large family, and they all lived in different houses built on the same premises. Benjamin couldn't remember the family being this large but that was almost thirty years ago. The seer had married two more wives as he had become richer due to the success of his predictions and fees for student tutoring. And that was not to mention his medicinal preparations which were now worth small fortunes. But there were many mouths to feed and every incoming dime mattered a lot. All the residents of the large compound settlement rushed to greet him and offered to unload the truck. The delightful look on their faces showed their enthusiasm and joy to receive their guest. A few seconds later as they were unloading the truck, the seer's assistant came to Mr. Strata and beckoned to him that the seer would see him now. As he entered the living room, Benjamin Strata noticed the well-furnished and spacious room with crosses of all sizes on the walls. There were two women sitting opposite the large HD TV across the room and as he passed by they both looked up at him and greeted him in one of the local Calazari dialects. Benjamin answered and guessed they must be the new younger wives of the seer. The assistant then beckoned him to follow him into one of the inner rooms which was detached from the house altogether. This was the office of the seer and as he entered, the old man was propped up on an adjustable leather chair which also served as a rocking chair at times. The old man greeted him and smiled at him as Benjamin bowed his head and hugged him affectionately.

"It has been a long time Benji," was the first statement he made. "So sorry I have heard about my daughter, your wife Maraya. Please take heart." At those words, Benjamin burst out sobbing like a child. "She was the best thing in my life, Papa. The best thing God ever gave me and the wicked ones have taken her away from me. What a wicked world." And that was the reply from Benjamin.

"Do not weep my son. Conserve your strength for there is a great battle ahead. And you must prepare the way for the one who will fight it and achieve victory. The enemy waits patiently for our unguarded hour to strike. My daughter was not watching; because I told her to come and see me at least once every three years but I last saw her twenty years ago. That was when you were in line to become the CEO of your company. I see you are the chairman now, but it was all because of the work we put in here that it all became possible and even reality. There is much work to do, much wisdom to possess." Benjamin tried to interrupt but the old man stopped him with a wave of his hand and then the seer continued.

"My son I have but a short time left here but let me speak and you must understand. I shall speak in parables so no evil bird picks up our words. I will tell you all you need to know and I will hand you over to my successor who will continue with you when I'm gone." Benjamin sat back in his chair and produced a small writing pad and a pencil and got ready to take notes.

"First, there is a battle that involves you, of which you may not be aware. There is a battle for the heart and the soul of this nation. Whoever holds the throne long enough to establish lasting power, whether light or darkness, will own the soul of the country. Evil has almost taken over Cretania. It even walks unopposed these days."

"Second, you remember almost thirty years ago when you and Maraya came here to inquire of your first son. If you can remember, he has been chosen to lead this battle and rekindle the lost glory of the nation and its people. You are a target because of your son's destiny. You have been chosen to bring the child who will restore light to Cretania. You are his fore-runner as his father and you must do many great things to prepare the way for him to succeed. If you fail, you have only guaranteed your son's failure. Maraya should be here to strengthen you in your task, but sorry the enemy has taken her. I must warn you Benji, do not fail. Maraya has failed and you can see the results. This is the great destiny of the Strata family. They have been watching you and you may not even know. But there's more I have to reveal."

"Third, you know this election and the one after it, they will be important in determining the struggle for the soul of Cretania. After the next election you will become a key member of the new government but that government will not last. Within its complete cycle, it shall be disrupted by the princes who rule over the country. They shall cast down stones to crush the queer ones and then the people of the princes shall cause the sea to rumble and there will be great trouble. In that trouble, the ruling king will be removed from the throne and be chased out of his beautiful mansion. He shall leave the nation never again to return. In that madness, your star will rise and the star of the House of Strata will shine brightly, but for a moment. But in that brief moment you must set up the path to the throne for the chosen one, your son Nino. This must be done so that he shall return after escaping the sword of the Pentosi and the Queen of Darkness. Then he will walk the path prepared for him to ascend the throne after the war. The queen and her king will take the throne by manipulation.

But her king will also hold it for only a short while; and then she shall seize power. They will seek to quench the light in the land and they will prosper but not completely. When the queen takes power she will linger on the throne, performing dark mysteries and terrible wickedness. But she will be removed from the throne by the power of the Most High. All this you must do and after your task will be complete. Make sure you and all your people are far away from Cretania by the time these evil two take power after the election. And know this—the queen and her king shall take power after your reign ends." The old man paused for Benjamin to finish writing and catch up with him. "Don't worry Benjamin. The God of heaven will give you the wisdom to succeed in your tough task. And he will cause you to have great favor so that the powers of Cretania will fight for you and save you and your son."

"Now finally, understand the powers that have arisen against the House of Strata. In the House of Nestel from which Maraya was from there is a black cat with many lives; and this is the one the external enemies use to destroy people and virtues in the family. The external enemies, even the princes of Cretania, have contacted the strongmen in both houses and these strongmen have in turn contracted internal enemies in both your houses. Your main external enemy is a brother in The Society, a hidden thorn in your flesh. In Maraya's family, the internal enemy is a woman who seems to never grow old. The secret to her unending youth is the blood of virgins. Separate her from those and she will die within seven days. Her death will mean the freedom of not only your two houses but also vengeance for the death of Maraya. And that's not to mention the countless virgins whose lives will be spared. As for your family, the internal destroyer is a man who derives power from the strongman himself. His weakness is his love for money and once you destroy him, the power of the strongman against you would be destroyed as well. Entice him with money that he may fall and do you no more harm. Then there will be peace in your family and a clear pathway for you and your son to achieve your goals with one less mortal enemy."

On hearing those words, Benjamin thought of asking how to entice this person with money so that he or she could fall. But as fast as the thought came to him he remembered how his own father had destroyed one of his half-brothers who threatened to kill him and all his family with voodoo. In a moment of desperation and fearing for the safety of his family, his father, Dr. Spencer Strata, had sent him a box full of raw cash, through a courier, as a peace offering. His uncle loved money so much that on seeing the 1 million US dollars he was ready to forgive and forget. But as he counted the money he had a massive heart attack and stroke and died within one minute of touching the raw cash. The money had been carefully laced with three different kinds of poisons including cyanide. The courier who had been waiting outside in his car came back about ten minutes later and found the body of the dead man. And the courier put on his gloves and collected all the money and left. That was how his father had saved his family and now it was his turn to save his own family from more dangerous and powerful enemies. History was simply repeating itself and he was wise enough to discern it.

"The God of heavenly wisdom will give you the wisdom you need to destroy your enemies and win your battles seeing that they are hard assignments from the heavens," Papa Mateo interrupted his deep thoughts.

"Thank you ever more, Papa," was the only reply from Mr. Strata after the speech from the old man. "Now you must meet Antonio, my son and assistant. He will take over this work when I am gone. There will be many of them but he will be their leader as he is the eldest of my sons and by far the most experienced." As he finished speaking, the two men stood up and approached each other and shook hands exchanging pleasantries in the process. After the exchange, Benjamin thanked the old man while simultaneously placing the boxes of money on the table by his side. The old man thanked him very much and bid him goodbye. The son-cum-assistant, Toni, escorted Benjamin back to his car and stood by, watching Mr. Strata and his entourage disappear into the distance under the warm evening sun.

CHAPTER FOUR

The Days of Reckoning

Nino woke up in the Intensive Care Unit, ICU, of the Shiloh General Hospital three days later. The doctors came in and informed him what had happened. He asked if Mona was still alive and the doctors told him she had no chance of survival. He felt so sorry because he didn't understand why he would kill his own wife. One of the nurses who knew who he was showed him a copy of one of the daily newspapers, *Shiloh Times*, published three days ago, and Nino read the article on what had happened to him. The article said that a top manager at the local Oil and Gas Company had strangled his wife to death while sleepwalking. Even though the paper didn't mention his name, he knew there were many in Shiloh who knew it was him. Nino was a completely broken man and felt he had no more reason to live. He desperately hoped his wife was not dead. When he was informed by the police that Mona had been stabbed five times in her chest causing the rupture of the main central blood vessels he became faint. The main artery in the neck and chest, the aorta, and the atria of the heart had been ruptured. Due to the strangeness of the situation, the police couldn't yet pin first degree murder charges on Nino. But his wife's death had been declared probable manslaughter, and he was the primary suspect. They still had him down for homicide and some of their best detectives were pressing for culpable murder charges. The enemies of the Strata family were all pressing for murder charges. And the maid Lena was a secondary suspect but had been removed from the list after DNA analysis so he was the only one left. Nino was afraid because he could recall that he had tried to strangle his wife but knew he had never tried to stab her before–not even when he was sleepwalking. He was terrified of the path his life would take now. The DNA analysis of samples taken at the crime scene would confirm whose blood it was that killed his wife. Meanwhile, the doctors had told him his level of depression was so high that his vitals were a major concern as they were at dangerously abnormal levels. So they kept him on admission in the hospital till further notice. The police was constantly coming in and out of the room and they had put him on suicide watch at the counsel of the psychologist. He knew his family was well connected if this case went to court and that would help him. But Mona's family was also well connected and a case as high profile as this will be hard to acquit even if he is not found guilty. The Spitzum family were not only influential but were also beloved by the people of Shiloh. Mayor Luther Spitzum who was the patriarch of the family just two generations ago was regarded as the best mayor the city ever had. And besides, the name Spitzum was generally associated with men and women with the gift of righteous and prosperous leadership. And now many will see him as a murderer of a member of such an illustrious and beloved family. He couldn't rule out assassination attempts on his life as the family were friends and acquaintances with mobsters and ruthless government officials. He knew now that only the most powerful of all beings could really save him now. That was if he was well enough, and not dead, by the time the case went to court.

While in that hospital room Nino couldn't stop pondering many things over and over in his head. When he was young he believed he had many powers as he could fly from place to place in a jiffy and from one country or continent to another in an instant. Where was all that power now? And why has all that power not been able to save him from these issues and problems that have appeared in his life and family. He could afflict, and had afflicted, those who offended him. On at least one occasion he had used his powers to destroy. And how come he was going through all this suffering from problems pouring in from every corner of the globe it seemed? He felt the world closing in on him and knew he was dying. But he couldn't save himself.

"Witchcraft is nothing but a foolish and powerful delusion which makes people believers in the falsehood that they were invincible and untouchable," Nino swore under his breath. He felt all that was happening to him wasn't supposed to happen—certainly not to a senior man of power like himself. Or even to his mother, as he began to recall her loving kindness and her hold on power. The most powerful spirits in Cretania had assured them death will not come until they all grew old and gray-haired. Now he knew better that the devil was nothing but a grand deceiver and the greatest liar. "The grand agenda of evil powers like witchcraft was to get as many as possible to hell." This was Nino's final thought as he noticed his temperature had begun to rise. He stopped the thoughts flowing and forced himself to go to bed with a heart filled with remorse.

The doctors came in the next day to talk with him and he was proven right. They told him his vitals were getting worse and all the treatments they had prescribed were not working for him. His prognosis was bad indeed. To make matters worse, they had found in an electrocardiogram and other heart tests that his heart had enlarged to almost one and a quarter times its normal size. They told him if it continued he would die in about two to three months. Nino seemed to be slowly waking up to one of the harshest realities of life.

"The day of reckoning will one day come for everyone," his thoughts began to run wild again. One night the head nurse for the medical ward, Simone King, came to see Nino in his room before she left for the night to cheer him up. As they spoke, he interrupted her to confide in her an important matter. "Nurse," he said, "I believe I know why I am suffering so much and maybe dying. I know you are a born-again Christian and I need to confide in you. There is one of my classmates in high school I did something terrible to long time ago. At this point he had begun to shed a few tears. I did something terrible and one of my high school girlfriends died. Her name was Ninita and I keep seeing her in my dreams calling me from the grave. It's terrible and I am so sorry for it but it won't go away but keeps tormenting me. One of us had to die, nurse. It was either she or me and I had no choice. It's just the nature of the dark world — nothing is gained without something. Please, nurse, help me and pray for me. I am losing my mind or something."

"Don't worry, Nino. Although murder is a wicked sin, Jesus is merciful, and he is willing to forgive you for all your sins if you confess them and repent and give your heart and soul to him. Make Jesus your Lord and Savior," Simone preached to Nino. "And someday," she whispered to him, "try to make restitution to the girl's family no matter how hard it may be. I promise you your secrets are safe with me. They all say you killed your wife but I feel in my heart that you are not the guilty one. But you must pray to Jesus, Nino. There are wicked powers trying to destroy you and only he can save you. I can tell you that as I was praying last night, I saw the image of a woman with a knife beside your wife as you were both asleep. It may be the same powers that made you a sleepwalker that are trying to set you up for this crime. But you know what Nino, it is the Lord who has permitted this to happen to you and your family so that you will change your ways and fear him and fulfill your destiny." On her way out Nurse Simone gave him a Bible and a few Christian tracts and books to read to cheer him up. She then asked him if he wanted a prayer before she left. He agreed, and she prayed as hard as she could for him for fifteen minutes and then she left. That night as he read the tracts and the Bible, tears began to fall from his eyes and he couldn't restrain himself from crying.

Days later, the police detectives from the Shiloh Police Department Homicide Unit who were put in charge of the case came into Nino's room to speak with him. They informed him that the DNA analysis was negative for his DNA. His blood, hair and fingerprint samples matched none of those retrieved from the crime scene. The SPD and criminal prosecutors were completely baffled. Nino's attorneys had warned him not to say a word to the police or attorneys for the Spitzum family so as not to jeopardize his case. The cause of death of Mona Spitzum-Strata had been ruled by the coroner's office as "Shock due to loss of blood as a result of the rupture of vital blood vessels and heart tissue caused by the repeated stabbing with a sharp weapon." The coroner had ruled out death by choking and asphyxiation as the COD. Hence, the choking pressure by Nino was considered not responsible for Mona's death. As a result, the case against Nino was getting weaker even though it was still a little strong. And the case for his innocence and acquittal was growing stronger every day. Because of this, Nino's attorneys could request Nurse Simone to arrange visitations for more Christians to come over to the hospital to minister to, and pray for, him. His request was granted in a few days' time and, though under tight security, Simone had just the perfect guest to see and pray for Nino.

Two days later during visiting hours Nurse Simone came in beaming with a smile. "I have great news for you, Nino. You know Jehovah answers prayers and he has answered ours," she told him smiling. "What could it be, please tell me nurse I really need it." "First, though your wife is dead all the experts have released a statement that it was not you but someone else that stabbed your wife to death. Closed-circuit TV street video showed what looked like an elderly woman leaving your home at about the same time as the crime. You are no longer the primary suspect I hear." Nino was speechless for the next sixty seconds. Then he burst out rejoicing. "O thanks to Jesus. What a relief," he replied with a sense of absolute joy.

"Second, your vitals have begun to stabilize, and you are now responding to treatment very well. So let's hope that whatever is causing the nightmares and sleepwalking should, hopefully, be a thing of the past soonest," the nurse continued to inform him. "Does that mean I will not die after all? If it is, then that's the greatest news and thanks so much. What amazing grace but I am still so afraid." He began to tear up quietly as she continued while holding his hands and saying "It's OK Dr. Strata. I assure you that you will not die."

"And finally, I have a special guest here to see you. She is a special friend and sister of mine and I believe you know her. Her name is Mimi Joy." "I don't believe I know that name, nurse," Nino replied. "It's a big surprise for you, Dr. Strata. Wait until you see her. Let me bring her to you." Those were Simone's final words as she turned to leave the room. "Okay," Nino replied in submission.

The lady was well-dressed wearing a well-tailored navy-blue ladies suit, and she stood about 5 feet 9 inches tall. At first, Nino couldn't place the face and then suddenly it clicked. It was Mimi Pockets from secondary school and he couldn't recognize her at first because her face had changed a lot after about twenty years.

"Hello Nino." Mimi spoke first and then ran and hugged him warmly. "Hello Mimi, longest time. How have things been with you all these years?" "I have been well, thanks Nino." "Are you married now, Mimi? I see your name has changed." "No, Nino. I changed it to be more in tune with my faith." It was now that Mimi went straight to the point. "Nino the reason I have come is that I heard what you were going through with your family and your health. And you know it is quite interesting that Simone and I attend the same church and she mentioned you in our prayer group when your ordeal began. You have suffered so much and the Lord Jesus Christ wants to save you from all your sufferings. Do you remember how I and Vivian spoke to you about salvation in Jesus?" Mimi asked him.

"It's been about seventeen years exactly this month, Mimi. I have never forgotten because it was so important to me. Once, I tried to reach you many years ago when my health problems began but I changed my mind." "Nino, I will remind you of all I told you back then 'cos nothing has changed. Jesus is the same yesterday, today and forever. He loves you, created you and wants you to come to him even now. Please don't resist him as you did many years ago." "I am ready now, Mimi. I have suffered too much. I am so sorry for all the evil I have ever done. And I am so sorry for rebuffing you in school many years ago. What do I need to do?" "You must accept Jesus as Lord and Savior by reciting the prayer of salvation. That action will make him your Lord and Savior. But first I must ask you: do you believe Jesus is the son of Almighty God and he came from heaven and died for your sins?" "Yes I do, my friend." "Excellent, Nino, and now you must repeat after me." Nino repeated the prayer of salvation after Mimi and in about thirty seconds he was finished and now a born-again Christian. He had never felt so much relief in his life. It was as though a giant burden was lifted off his shoulders and he began to weep like a baby. "Let me now pray for you, Nino," Mimi said after a few seconds of silence. Immediately after the prayer, he felt a cold feeling coming over him from his head moving over his body to the soles of his feet. "What you are feeling is the Holy Spirit, Nino. You need the Holy Spirit to live a Christian life. You must come to the church and join us and become a member of the ministry. The name of the ministry is Mount Zion Pentecostal Ministry and I will leave you the church address here on this card. When you come you will begin the Anointing Ministry which is the deliverance programme. That will rid you of all these myriad problems you are having and set you free to begin to live for Jesus." "I will be there once I leave this hospital and have recovered at home."

As Mimi turned to leave, Nino called out to her in a soft tone, "Mimi can I confide in you?" "Yes of course," she replied. "Do you remember Ninita from secondary school? She died when we were in Class 4. If I had something to do with her death will you still be my best friend?" Mimi smiled at him with sympathy. "Nino the Bible says that 'when a man is born again he is a new creature; old things are past and all things are become new.' Jesus has forgiven you and now you must forgive yourself."

"Mimi, Ninita was evil and she tried to harm me and I had to do something about it before she did. Believe me that's the truth," Nino spoke as though he was sorry. "You see, Mimi, it's the madness of darkness. Her people tried to use her as a lamb and in her desperation to survive, she tried to exchange with me. Do you understand?" Nino spoke pleading for sympathy. "Well Nino, I have a little confession of my own," Mimi began to tell Nino a strange story.

"On the night Ninita died I had a vision about that time and I saw two dark male figures going to her home. And I saw one of them thrust a short sword into her chest while she slept. As the two males left the scene of the crime I saw both of their faces. It was you and Skinny, was it not? And it was you who plunged the sword. The vision was so clear that night. It is more than coincidence that my visions were in the right place and the right time. It must be that we share a common destiny. And let me assure you I never stopped praying so hard for you since that night so that this matter might not destroy you. Her blood cries out against you so hard that all heaven and hell can hear her cry. And now that you have repented from every sin, the blood of Jesus will silence every blood crying against you. That's why you lost your mind and almost died. Since your destiny, I mean our destiny, is so great, the Lord has kept you alive all these years that we may fulfill this great destiny together. So I warn you, my dear friend, you must get close to Jesus and begin to serve him so you can begin to fulfill your great destiny. I am surprised you don't know this, Nino. Ninita's father is a high-ranking occultist and I heard he swore to get his revenge on whoever killed his only daughter. But guess what? It was he who killed Ninita. Because it was he who possessed you every time you had sex with his wife. Yes, Nino, I know you slept with his wife. He was the one behind it all. He controlled your spirit and sent you to kill his daughter so he could use her for blood money rituals. And after that he claimed it was you who killed Ninita and that you must die for your crime. He must have sent evil spirits or occult powers to cause these problems. I believe that is why you are here now. And finally Nino let me warn you—if you don't belong to Jesus, they will destroy you. And that's because they are too powerful for you, dear friend. Mr. Thorn is on one of the highest levels in the black occult. Please do not play with this matter. They have seen your star Nino, and they know who you are and are out to destroy you. Destruction of this society is what Thorn and people like him seek to do as commanded by their father, Satan. And people like us were sent by God, our Heavenly Father, to save it."

Nino's eyes lit up with fire. "O God of gods, who will not fear you? You have placed greatness in the hands of commoners, and you have given the lives of the mighty into the control of lowest. This is too much for me. Mimi, are you my mother and I never even knew it? God Almighty has made you a mother and god to me," Nino said quietly but in obvious shock. "My life is in your hands Mimi," Nino finally said as he lay down on the hospital bed feeling overwhelmed by the situation.

"I assure you Nino, your life is mine and mine is yours and we are both in the hands of God. I promise you that as long as the sun rises from the east and sets in the west, neither this thing nor any of your other secrets will ever get into enemy hands. The Lord will save you from the many beasts pursuing you, be sure of that. So long, and do get some peaceful sleep." As she left, she bent over him and planted a kiss on his forehead. As Mimi left the room, Nino was already falling asleep.

A few days later the doctors came and confirmed that Dr. Nino Strata was well and fully recovered. And they declared him well enough to be discharged to go home. A few days after, all the security arrangements by the SPD were in place.

Nino was to be placed under 24-hour watch and confined to house arrest once he got home.

The day before his discharge from the hospital was a Sunday, and it was the last day of the month. He was under strict legal restrictions but Nino was still so happy that he was leaving the hospital alive. Every day in the hospital had become quite typical—early morning Christian devotion after waking up from a peaceful sleep. But today was different as he had woken up from a terrifying nightmare. It was a dream that began with six hooded figures all pointing at him. Soon after, three of them changed to wolves while the other three changed to lions and they all began pursuing him. Nino turned and ran as fast as he could but the animals were soon catching up to him. As the fastest of the lions were about to pounce on him Nino ran into a house for safety. He woke up from sleep sweating and breathing heavily. Then he glanced at the time on the clock on the wall in front of his bed. It was exactly 6:30 a.m., and he reached for the water jug on the table beside his bed and drank all its contents. He then cleaned off the sweat on his face and body. At the same time, he looked out the window of his room in the medical ward where he had been transferred from the ICU months ago. It was gearing up to be a gray day as there was no sign of the sun anywhere. On a normal Sunday at this time of the year the morning sun would be out by this time and blazing hot too. A few seconds later there was a knock on the main room door.

Shortly after, the large door flung wide open to reveal an elderly lady somewhere in her mid-sixties standing at the entrance of the door. She walked in and before Nino could protest, she was standing by his bedside. The first thought that came to his mind was that one of his enemies or his father's enemies had sent an assassin to kill him. The Spitzum family was his first suspect as he knew they would never give up on their quest for revenge.

"O Lord, if I will die now let it not be in the hands of a woman. Not an old, fearsome and ghostly looking woman for that matter. What a laughingstock the Strata family would be," Nino prayed silently. He thought of his poor father and what would happen to him with his wife and now his first son gone so soon. But he probably deserved it anyway considering the way Mona died and all she suffered. He had prepared his mind for this moment for a long time since his father had become such a powerful and wealthy politician. And he too had risen to such great prominence. In Cretania, the slightest bit of success attracted a wide range of enemies from all spheres of the society. "How will this be," he thought to himself. "O death, suffer me not and just make this quick."

As he continued watching her, he noticed she was carrying a medium-sized picture frame in one hand and a 5-foot long shepherd's rod in her other hand. She didn't look familiar to him but there was something about her presence that both comforted and terrified him at the same time. On close observation, Nino noticed she was dressed as a nurse and assumed she was one of the nurses he had never met. It was at this point he changed his mind about her. This woman was no assassin or else she would have initiated real deadly action by now. It was then he guessed she might be a visitor who was familiar with his family. Perhaps she was a friend of his father or late mother who had come to see him to say hello and wish him speedy recovery and present him with gifts. He heaved a sigh of relief at this thought.

His eyes then shifted from her personality and dressing back to what she was carrying. He then noted that the painting had five separate paintings all on this one painting canvas. There was a centrally located one which took up most of the space on the canvas. And then all the others were smaller paintings that were firmly positioned in the northern, southern, eastern and western portions of the canvas in relation to the main centrally located one. They were all the same brightness and clarity, like as though they were videos recorded in high definition.

"Hello my dear son. I am a friend so please don't be afraid." She must have read his mind. Nino concluded that she was definitely not an assassin. The voice of his spirit calmed his troubled soul by convincing him that she was a friend. There was so much power in her presence and even more when she spoke. Her voice sounded musical but dry and hoarse just like the unending echo of a rhythm guitar playing slowly on a hot and humid sunny day. She had droopy eyes and as she spoke her eyes focussed on the eyes of her subject. The look was that of a sharp sword cutting deep into the soul with every word and thought. Her first few words started a chain reaction in his soul and it was like a dead object that had been brought to life after being dead for a long time. One part after the other was coming alive. As the strange cold feeling overwhelmed him he realized it was time for him to speak back to the strange woman.

"My name is...," Nino began to say but was quickly interrupted by the stranger. "I know your name, Dr. Nino Strata, and I know who you are. You are the first child and first son of Benjamin and Maraya Strata. All hell has broken loose against you and your family but you must not be afraid and do not worry. You will survive and give great testimony about it all. But you must listen and understand all I will tell you now and obey every single instruction. Now you must listen carefully as we don't have much time." As she spoke, Nino was speechless and found he was powerless to interrupt her speech or even move his body.

"I have been sent to show you your destiny and power in the great journey on which you are about to embark. You will have a rod and a staff to empower you. And you will have a great helper to complement, complete and strengthen you all your days. I have in my hands a medium-sized painting and a 5-foot rod. Take them as I explain to you what they are." At this point she handed both the stick and the canvas to him. He quickly put them by his side on the bed and kept on watching and listening to her totally transfixed on her.

"Look upon the painting and tell me what you see?" She asked him. "I see a painting of a wooden cross with Jesus Christ crucified in the center of the canvas," he replied. "Well done, you have seen well. Now understand that at the beginning of the journey that is what you will see on the picture canvas. The powers of darkness wish to cast down the glory of the highest of all gods in this nation and bring him great shame and dishonor. But that will never happen. The almighty Creator of the universe has sent me to show these things to you. He is the reason you are still alive to begin this journey. And he is the reason you will overcome all obstacles, win all battles and reach the expected end of the journey. It's all about him and the glory of his kingdom. This is the Lord's battle and not yours. You must never forget that. This is also the same painting you will also see at the end of your destiny when the journey's done and it's time to return home. At the beginning as at the end the cross will be the only painting on the canvas." She then paused for a while to study the look on his face; and after about ten seconds she turned her gaze back to the canvas and continued.

"After this time and between the beginning and the end you will see many other images. At the center will be the paintings of your immediate divine agenda. It will only appear in emergencies or urgencies. To the north of the central painting will be the evil plots and events against you and the powers and people who are behind them. In the south will be the paintings of each way you can avoid all the evil being plotted against you. Thus, in the south you will find your escape plan which must be followed diligently. The west is where there will be the paintings that show the next step to be taken in the journey. God's will for your journey, whether you should go left rather than right or take west rather than east, will be made clear in the western images. Understand that the sun rises in the east and sets in the west. So the east is where you are coming from and the west is where you are going. And as for the east you will find all the paintings of all past events. It is where you have been and from where you are coming. You will have as many helpers as you need. The most important helper will be your wife. She will strengthen you and help you along this journey even unto the glorious end."

"As for the rod, you should have it as a companion with you in all the places you go when battles, or your enemies, are waiting. It will keep you against your enemies, and also in battle." As she finished speaking she laid her right hand on his right shoulder and gave him what was perhaps the most important of all the instructions. At this point there was a knock on the hallway door and Nino thought it was one of the nurses coming for her rounds as usual. The stranger did not as much as turn to look at the direction of the main door. She continued speaking in her usual tone.

"Finally, you must never disclose this matter to anyone. The picture must be hidden away in your innermost place. And you must never return to your former ways of darkness, never. If you obey in all these things you will be victorious."

Immediately she spoke her last words, she turned and walked towards the balcony door and she was gone. Nino was still dazed and confused by all that had happened. It must have been the power of her presence more than all the information she had given him. The next day he was discharged from Shiloh General Hospital.

When he got home, he met only Lena the maid. He inquired of her whether Mona's mother had been there recently and the maid said she had no idea. Lena also didn't know if Mona's body had been cremated or buried. If not yet, he wondered when they would be done. Nino discovered that Mona's mother, Monica, came by five weeks earlier and she left certain documents for him to read. Nino did not have the strength to look in the envelope or read its contents until the next day after his evening dinner. The contents were documents which he read with great amazement. It was Mona's funeral plans but it had stated clearly that Nino wasn't invited. The pressure from the Strata family about the barrenness, the health issues in Nino's family and his sleepwalking had already destroyed the marriage. The Spitzum family thought it was better to end the marriage after one whole decade of childless marriage between Nino and Mona. But they wanted to break the news to Nino at the weekend get-together having no idea a greater news, the death of their daughter, awaited them. Old feelings of guilt and sorrow were overwhelming him again. A voice inside him told him to let the feelings and her memory go but he couldn't. After a few days he felt it was the power of Ninita's father getting to him again. But then that voice told him to pray about it and after a couple of hours of resisting he decided to get on his knees and pray. Nino cried to the Christian God, Jesus, from the bottom of his heart. It was like a man who seemed to be okay on the outside but was decaying to death inwardly. His world had come to an end on the inside and he knew it. This was confirmed by the battle going on inside his head—a battle between light and darkness.

There were too many voices talking in his head and most of them were talking him into his grave. There was the voice of Mr. Thorn accusing him of killing "his Ninita." There was the voice of Mona's family accusing him of killing their daughter and sister. And there were the voices of the so many people who believed he was a murderer, whether it was for the death of Ninita or his wife Mona. And of course there were the voices and images of Mona and Ninita tormenting him constantly. These were the voices on the side of darkness. On the light side there were only two voices. There was the voice of his dear friend Mimi reassuring him with the so many comforting words that everything will be OK. And there was a soft, gentle and persistent voice telling him to be strong and have no fear. It was the voice of God's spirit and Nino knew it. It was an experience that would forever imprint on his heart that whatever the troubling situation, God would always be there for him. After about two hours of prayer he felt so much better and the painful throbbing headache that was tormenting him all day finally went away. That night as he prepared for bed he began to imagine what the court procedure would be like and what would happen to him. But then he remembered Mimi telling him how much Jesus loved him and would forgive him if he truly repented of his sins. Nino's predominant thought was that maybe Jesus would help him get acquitted. And he also remembered when Mimi told him how important his destiny was.

As he began to fall sleep, he said out loud "I truly repent Lord Jesus, I truly repent. Please forgive me for I really wish to achieve this great calling you have for me. I really do, and if you will help me throughout my life, I will obey you and serve you forever." And then as he drifted in and out of sleep he heard the voice of his father calling him. As usual he at once found himself in the "Vineyard," which was the nickname of the family coven in his paternal home town. His father asked him how he was doing and he replied that he believed he would get better. But Nino was afraid of death and all the events that had happened. Benjamin Strata informed his son why he had to stay away from him during this period. He explained that due to his political affiliations and aspirations to federal office, his support of Nino would cause him serious political problems and could be tantamount to political suicide. Nino understood quite well how politics worked and especially in Cretania where the slightest public blunder could end even the strongest political ambitions or careers.

"I am working hard to get you out of this mess my dear son just hang in there," Benjamin reassured his first son. "Okay father, I will be hopeful and thanks," Nino replied as he hugged his father. As soon as his father left, Nino returned to his home. A few days later, the police surveillance and house arrest were canceled and called off permanently.

CHAPTER FIVE

Arrows from Afar

The wind was blowing at about 12 miles per hour in the direction of West Northwest. Fog was medium-light and visibility was about 15 meters. Outside temperature in the town that night, as with the past two nights, ranged between 6 to 9 degrees Celsius. It was quite strange to be this cool at this time of the year which was September in the third quarter of the year. The normal temperature should have been about 15 degrees Celsius plus, but there was nothing normal about the town of Sepsis. Residents of the neighboring towns and villages saw the name of the town as a curse. The town began life with the name Ophir but that had changed. It was a small town and had exactly eighteen residents. It was rumored that six of its residents belonged to the devil and six belonged to the Antichrist while the remaining six belonged to the false prophet. But most Cretanians hardly believed that the devil had any presence in their country. The geopolitical lines that divided the town resulted in three regions—the North, the East and the West. Each of the divisions had six residents and all residents were institutions which were political, religious or financial. And some institutions were a combination of two or more of them. Each of the residents had a large building which was usually the headquarters of that organization in the state of Prophétie or the nation itself. The state of Prophétie was the northernmost state in the country south of the Capitol states and the town of Sepsis was right in the center of the state. Political representation occurred at the level of each of the town's divisions. The residents chose someone from their ranks to oversee their own region in political matters. It was perhaps the reason Sepsis never had a mayor. Or perhaps it was because no one dared ask for a mayor.

Going through or even near the town terrified many residents of the state. In fact, the name Sepsis was given when citizens suspected that the epidemic outbreak began here in the town. Some of the organizations in the town were believed to have produced the bacterial disease. Needless to say, it was one of the most hated and controversial places in the country. So as to forever etch the epidemic incident in memory, the state leaders changed the name of the town. The name Sepsis was born out of the infamy unleashed by the epidemic at local and national levels.

The irony of the Sepsis story was that the state had the reputation of being the home of the greatest number of spiritual and religious prophetic houses in Cretania. And therefore, things like an epidemic were never expected to occur, talk less originate, in the state. But the town of Sepsis had a dark and ugly history which few dared speak about, whether in public or in private, or rise up to challenge. There were few Cretanians who doubted that Prophétie was the center of the spiritual battle in the country. Many people believed that the most influential institutions in the town were the financial and religious ones. The most powerful financial institution was the Cretania First Bank while the most powerful religious one was the All Saints Church.

In the center of Sepsis stood the All Saints Church cathedral which was one of the most mysterious organizations not only in Sepsis but in

Cretania. It was a magnificent, gargantuan edifice built using architecture from the *Renaissance Era*. Its owners, clergy and presbytery were mostly unknown, preferring anonymity. But the church itself was the most prestigious of all churches in the country. This was because only the most powerful and richest citizens attended the church. And the only occasions of attendance was celebration or funeral of the same caliber of people.

The State of Prophétie was indeed the home of the prophets. It had a long history of being the state where many great prophets called home since the country's founding over 150 years ago. It was this prophetic mission that's believed to be responsible for producing generations of successful governments and prosperous economies. This, in turn, changed the fortunes of the continent. It was this change that led to the formation of nations in the continent of Yellow River. The most prominent nation was this one which they called Cretania. And it would become the model used to create all other nations in Yellow River. It was the prophets who gave the continent its name. It was the prophets who laid the foundation of the country, wrote the constitution and called the state 'prophecy' or Prophétie. The French name was chosen in honor of the state's Franco-prophetic origins. Every significant prophecy about anything or anyone since the founding of the country originated from the state. Whether they were concerning issues on the local, national or global scene, most prophecies were often given first by one of the prophets in Prophétie. Every highway that entered the state had a giant signboard that read: "*Bienvenue à l'état de Prophétie –La maison des prophètes de Cretania.*"

People believed that this was where God would raise and breed his prophets which he would use to determine the fate of the country and the continent. But here the country was 150 years after its founding. The country was now under the rule of despotic men and women, evil dictators and unrepentant tyrannical leaders. Worst of all, these evil people had infiltrated the home of the prophets in their brazen quest to destroy the prophetic legacy of Cretania. And now there were few prophets left, a number many put at thirty, give or take five. The sheer audacity of the evil that had struck Cretania was a great puzzle to everyone both religious and atheist alike.

And then one night, the night of the 18th of September, there was unusual silence throughout the town. As usual you could almost hear a pin drop at night. All visitors, clients and officials of the various organizations would have left the town by 9 p.m. This night was no different. But there was something strangely different about tonight. It was now about 11:45 p.m. when signs of life began to appear. At All Saints Church, the resident pastor, Pastor Clemency Donaldson, had instructed the groundskeeper, Vern, to lock all doors and gates. The keeper of the grounds had retired to his quarters near the back gates for the night. The pastor had retired to his suite on the upper floor. On the upper floor, which was also the highest floor in the cathedral, there were four suites arranged in a square floor plan. The pentagonal structure which housed the elevator served to divide and separate the suites. Pastor Donaldson's suite was opposite the elevator just across the large hall. Suite 'V & C', which was the visitor and conference suite, was on the right side of the elevator. And the suite of the

Lord Bishop of the All Saints Church was on the left side. The Lord Bishop, Peter Christos, hardly resided here preferring his sprawling mansion in the country side around Sepsis. But when he took residence, he wielded absolute authority over the church activities and staff, and total control over all church properties. But it was the suite behind the elevator that was the most mysterious of all the rooms in the church. It was the largest of all the suites and had the design of a mini-palace. It was like an ancient kingdom decorated with expensive but ancient furniture. The main living room was like a throne room fit for a great king. About thirty meters in front of the throne were five executive chairs. On the wall behind the throne was a large inverted cross painted in black.

By a few minutes to 12 a.m. the arrivals had begun. The occupants of the five chairs in front of the throne began arriving at ten minutes to midnight. Two of them arrived first and then the next two arrived four minutes later. Another three minutes later, the last one arrived. They all took their seats and were all seated before midnight. At exactly one minute to 12 a.m., a circle of twelve black crows entered the town's airspace and approached the cathedral. The circle had a thirteenth, and much larger, crow in the middle of the formation. They reached the cathedral in time to land on the ceiling over the throne suite with ten seconds left to midnight. As they landed on the ceiling, the first six entered through the ceiling into the suite while the middle crow went next and the remaining six followed. By the time they entered the throne room, the middle crow had transformed into a dark giant figure whose presence was as powerful as it was menacing. The figure proceeded to seat on the throne. All the other birds had transformed into lesser figures that surrounded the throne and its occupant. Once the avian contingent arrived, the five men who had arrived earlier all jumped to their feet like they were waiting for a lord or king. As the throne figure took his seat, they all resumed their positions seating down on their ancient chairs. As soon as they took their seats, the five chairs in the throne room bowed their heads down in unison. With heads bowed they all spoke at the same time: "Welcome, Great Master. We bow to the Great Zebulon, Lord of Cretania, King of the Cretan

Legions." The Master waved his hand, and they all sat down straight on their seats.

As usual the first chair was the most powerful of all the chairs in any meeting; and was the first and normally the last to speak during their meetings. After the first chair had spoken, then the second would speak. And then the third, fourth and the fifth chairs would speak. But that arrangement was binding only during the meetings and group rituals. The third chair was actually the executive chair. Its occupant was by far the most powerful of all the other occupants of the chairs. In times of emergency, only the third chair was allowed to address the meeting. After all chairs had finished speaking and giving their answers to their Master's questions, the Master would give a final speech and then end the meeting with no rituals. And this meeting took place once every six months in normal time and once every three months in war time or emergencies.

"Our Master has the room," were the first words spoken by any of the chairs since resuming their seats. It was the voice of the first chair, Chair 1. "Our Master has the room," was the encore of all the other chairs in one accord. The dark giant figure on the throne cleared his throat and began speaking.

"My worthy servants, it's been six months since our last meeting and so much has transpired between then and now. All our projects are still on course for successful completion. But there are few things I wish to remind you all about before we proceed with this final meeting for the year. First, I must remind you that you have all been carefully chosen as the greatest and most distinguished citizens of this great country. You have all come from generations of distinguished men and women servants of our high Lord, the King of Darkness himself, and, of course, my own self. Your ancestors have served many lords with diligence and unquestionable loyalty with some even dying in the line of service. So it is not a mistake that you find yourself here in this place." He paused for a while to look at all the figures seated on the chairs. He then continued.

"Second, I must say for the millionth time: we do not, and can't afford to, tolerate failure. The successful completion of all our projects is extremely vital to the continued stronghold and authority we wield in this country. This is important to ensuring the survival of our kingdom and people in Cretania. The slightest failure, even the perception of failure, will set us back many years and generations. It may even uproot us from this country altogether. You must organize your people to hold on to power. You must mobilize them so that we have all the information that enters, circulates or leaves this country. If a pin drops in Cretania we need to know because that's how we will hold on to power. We must not fail." He continued speaking after a short pause.

"Third, I need to re-emphasize the absolute virtue of silence in all our affairs especially about our projects. Never grant interviews or speak about anything to do with us, our projects, or our meetings. You are the rulers of this country, and you must rule well. Speak less and do more. Understand that the best speech you can ever give is silence. Our former Chair 3 did not understand that. And now he is paying the ultimate price for his betrayal of our trust."

"Finally, we know a strong wind has blown this way recently. It was a wind of enmity, flashes of lightning carried by the wind, a wind that threatens to destroy us and all our plans for this great land. It is a warning that our enemies in the highest places are on to us and plan to destroy our great plans. There are at least seventy of their messengers who have arrived in Cretania. We expect they will be watching us perhaps even now and we have our eyes on them as well. One of your tasks is to find out what they have done, are doing, and all those they have visited and the purpose of those visits. Their goals are obvious, but how do they plan to achieve them? The battle for Cretania is now reaching its climax. You all have much work to do."

"Now let us hear the update on all our projects except the sixth one. You all recall the sixth project is our main goal and is the culmination of all the other projects. That one will be strictly under my authority." As the Master finished speaking, he cast his piercing gaze on the first chair.

"Project Zombie is going on as planned and is running on schedule. The final results will be in about two years from now," the first chair answered. "Well done, Chair 1," the Master replied as he turned from the first chair to the figure in the second chair.

"Project Electorate is also going on as planned. We are close to our final destination and we are ready. So, we are ahead of the schedule given us," the figure in the second chair replied in confidence. "Well done, Chair 2. You will receive a good reward at the end of your project." After saying this, the Master turned to third chair.

"Project Cretania House is rolling ahead with full steam. We must deliver on our part but I have a question, my lord." "Speak, Chair 3," the Master replied impatiently.

"Now that Everlast has betrayed us, do we strike him out of all our dealings and from the entire project? And if he retaliates against us what do we do to him and his people seeing he is still such a powerful man with powerful friends and connections. We need to know what to do to him and how to deal with him."

"President Everlast is a dead man, you mark my words. We made him who he is and now he has bitten the hand that fed him and lifted up his head.

He will die and all his family will die with him—I swear it by the 'Lords of Death.' You don't worry about him and remove his name from all our records but make sure you neither confront nor provoke him. He is a cunning lion in battle so don't try to fight him now. We will render him powerless when you replace him. You just focus on your rise to power and replacing him." With those words the Great Master turned to the fourth chair.

"The Environ Project has had a few hitches recently but I am happy to report that all those problems are now resolved. In our traditional manner we have taken care of all who stood in our way. There are no loose ends and we have no problem meeting out scheduled deadline. All systems are 'go' for the timing of the great shower." The fourth chair spoke in a loud voice while starring into the dark fiery eyes of the Master.

"I have confirmed your report, and you have excelled. Keep up the great work; all our people hail your wisdom and resolve. But do we have an estimate?" the demon king asked. "Yes Master, we do. We shall have about six to ten and no less," the figure in the fourth chair replied. "We need every one. Well done, Chair 4. Well done," the demon king gave his congratulations. And finally the Master turned to the figure in the fifth chair.

"Project Intelligence has been working hard to cover the width and breadth of Cretania. And not only that we cover the whole continent and the whole world. We have every piece of information that is out there or in private about this country. And we have information about the world that concerns us. The president may have received word or may be about to soon. But we will know once he does for certain because we have two of our people who are close to him." The fifth chair paused for five seconds as if waiting for comments. He then continued.

"Lord, I am well aware of the holy ones who have come to fight for, and prepare the people who will fight for Cretania. We know they have chosen a young man from the state of Shiloh and two or more helpers with him. There are also three of their churches and ministries which support these chosen ones. But two of the churches we know well. And we have the identity of those we suspect and we must strike them now. Our intelligence points to three great houses and we have targeted them. Once we cut them off, we will alert this assembly."

"We have no time, Chair 5," the Master interrupted. "You and your people have the most abundant power besides the president in this country, so use it well. The next time we meet we must have all the details we need. And I do not want to call an emergency meeting just to alter other plans due to your failure. Is that understood Chair 5?" The king was now getting irritated. "We have gone so much further than you have and we don't even dwell amongst you."

As he finished that statement, one of the spirits that sat on the right of the Legion King came near him and took something from his hands. He moved quickly over to Chair 5 and handed the package over to him. Chair 5 wrote the names of the houses of each of the three suspects on each item in the package and in turn handed them to Chair 1 and they all took their seats again.

"Yes, Great One, I understand perfectly," Chair 5 replied solemnly as he stared at the feet of the throne as if feeling sorry for himself.

By the time Chair 1 thanked the Great Master and all his contingent for their presence, a heavy downpour had begun over the town. By this time there was a thick cloud over the cathedral and from a distance what seemed to be ships in the clouds. Despite the rain, the Master and his entourage transformed back to black crows and vanished out of the roof into the rain. All the chairs left one after the other according to their rank. A little while after they all got out, Pastor Donaldson emerged from his room and went down to his office from where he summoned Vern. Vern rushed into the office of the pastor and took the package the pastor handed over to him.

"You know what to do, Vern?" the pastor asked him when he arrived just to be certain. Vern nodded and accepted the package. Vern hurried to the top of the building and went to a cage where there were six ravens asleep. He took three of the birds and put one of the three items from the cloth on each raven. He then took the ravens out of the cage and released them into the air watching them disappear into the foggy sky as the church bells started ringing. At the same time he walked into the balcony of the cathedral facing into the church and backing the balcony. He shouted into the empty church, "The arrows have flown, the arrows have flown." It was as though he could see people in the empty seats as he spoke with his eyes dotting from one side of the church to the other. As he finished speaking he looked at the cathedral clock and he noticed it was 6 a.m. and dawn would soon break in Sepsis. The birds had flown off and had climbed to an altitude of about 10,000 feet.

On the outskirts of the town at its border with the neighboring city of Lyon, an elderly woman stood behind an abandoned kiosk watching the cathedral and the events unfolding within. She quickly returned to the boat that was waiting on the river below the adjoining bridge. In the boat there were four other persons waiting for her and looking towards the same direction of the cathedral. They started the boat and drove away.

As they drew away from the city of Sepsis, the only woman in the group looked at the ravens as they flew away towards the south for a considerable distance. Then she turned her gaze to her colleagues one by one and then she turned to the one nearest to her. His eyes were still following the birds as they flew at a steady pace following a direction southbound. Later, each bird started to drift apart, and they all began flying towards different paths. The bird watcher kept on watching as another colleague joined in the watch. And they kept on watching till the birds were separated and were now flying in three different directions. They had also noticed that each of the birds was color-coded on the top of its head and on its beak. They had been flying for about thirty nautical miles when it became clear where each one of them was heading. The one that flew on the left after its release had adjusted its flight path and was now flying towards a direction west southwest at the same altitude. This suggested it was flying towards the western parts of the state of Shiloh. This bird had the color red on its head and beak. The second raven which was in the middle when released was now flying in the direction of true south. But it had increased its altitude by about 7,000 feet suggesting it was flying over Shiloh and either heading for the states of Calazar or Western River in the southwest of Cretania. It had the color blue on its beak and head. The third bird was on the right after release and was flying on a straight path to the southeast. It had the color purple on its head and beak. It had also increased its altitude by about 5,000 feet which indicated it was flying east of the Yellow River either to Happyness or Portland.

The men and the woman on the sail boat understood so well what the flight was about and all that was going on. All members of the group knew every destination to which the birds were heading. They also knew the full identity of the targets of the birds and their deadly cargo. It was obvious the birds were headed for the cities of Summit in Calazar, Goldport in Portland and Shiloh in the state of Shiloh. As the birds finally flew out of sight of the monitoring group, they congratulated themselves at the successful confirmation of the destination of the flight birds. And they wasted no time in proceeding to the next phase of the task before them.

"Now we have confirmed where our little feathery harbingers of death are traveling to we must spare no time in beating them to it. Thank God they chose birds and not something more challenging." It was the woman who spoke first. "That's true," all the men answered in unison.

"So we all know what to do now. Both of you must go to the Grinders in Calazar. Just to make certain Jacob does not return or show up during this period." The mystery lady was speaking to the two men on her left side. And they both nodded in response. "The two of you should hasten to the House of Strongbow in Goldport." This time she was speaking to the other two men who were on her right side. And they both answered "okay" at the same time. "I must hurry to Mimi and her great friend. After the battles we must reunite in the next meeting place. Then we will tackle the plans of the Pentosi and The Society to unleash terrible evil on this nation. If for any reason there is a change to our plans, however slight, let one signal all. We must meet again in twenty-one days by our Lord's grace."

As they finished speaking, the boat was brought to a stop inside a boat storehouse which housed only one boat at a time. They all alighted from the boat and went into an inner room, closing the gates of the boat house behind them to make sure that no one interrupted them. As they entered the inner room and closed its door behind them they formed a queue in the order of their assignments. The woman brought up the rear behind the two pairs of men. After one man in the first pair hit the wall once and screamed "sortir," a large geopolitical map of the country appeared on the wall before them. On this map the first pair of men located and pointed to the city to which they were traveling. And then a flash of light appeared and immediately disappeared into that city with the two men disappearing with it. The second pair of men did the same thing with their own assigned city and disappeared with the flash of light into their own city. And finally the woman did the same thing, disappearing with the light into the city of Shiloh. She appeared in Shiloh City, at a four-star hotel not far from the Mount Zion Pentecostal Church.

CHAPTER SIX

Resistance to Deliverance

At his first visit to Mount Zion Pentecostal, Nino met all those who had made his salvation possible. Mimi, Simone, their prayer group and Mimi's father and senior pastor Bishop Michael Pockets. They all welcomed him and after they all talked about his salvation and his unique situation, he registered for the deliverance program. On that day, he was baptized in water in the lake two kilometers from the church premises. The deliverance program would run for three months in total but the first and most crucial part was the first three weeks. It felt like a whole new start for Nino, and Mimi was there to keep him company and hold his hand. Mimi, he discovered, seemed to know everything about him and his life and this pleased him very much. Two weeks later the deliverance program began and within three weeks he had completed the most important part of the program. At the end of the deliverance ministration he made a great observation. Before the deliverance program,

Mimi had gone on and on about how important it was for him to receive his deliverance. "Without deliverance, there can be no holiness," she had said countless times. "And without holiness there can be no relationship with Jesus and then salvation is in vain." Nino had noticed that even though he was born again he could still leave his body and fly to all the places he desired. Nothing, it seemed, had changed. Until the deliverance program began. On the first day, many small, strange-looking birds came out of his body spontaneously and they were all dead. About the third hour on the first day as they prayed he noticed something happen to him for the first time. As he prayed to cut off all ties with witchcraft, he felt a powerful surge running through him. It felt like a bucket of cold water pouring down on him. It was overpowering but calming, and it was painful but soothing. He could no longer stand on his feet and found himself on the ground. When he came around, he noticed the spirit eyes he used to see into the spirit world were no longer there. He also saw the many birds that belonged to the powers on his father's and mother's sides had left him. As he continued to gather himself together, he looked up from the objects on the floor that left his body and saw a face. It was Mimi reassuring him that everything was going well. That was the end of the first day.

Similar things happened on the second and third days of the deliverance program. It was on the second day he noticed he couldn't leave his body any longer and while it dumbfounded him, it also surprised him in a pleasant way. It was then he understood the value of deliverance. And then the third day came and went and then three weeks passed so fast. All the bad dreams had stopped and the occasional chest pain including the depression were all gone. All the problems, health and all, seemed to have disappeared. He had to pray and fast for the three weeks during the program. He had never prayed so much and so hard in his life. Besides, he had never gone without food and fluids for such long periods. Nino had gone without food and water each day from 12 midnight to 7 p.m. It was tough but there was no turning back now. He recalled the words of Mimi and the strange woman in hospital and thought about his destiny. He felt it was all worth it and he was so pleased about it he couldn't wait to tell his dear Mimi. "What a bundle of joy Mimi Joy has been to me?" Nino wondered to himself.

But Nino had celebrated a little too early. By the time the third week came around there were many other strange things going on in his life. He noticed he couldn't reach most of his family members. "It was either that or they have all disappeared from the earth," was the thought that crossed his mind. Just as he was about getting worried there was news that one of his deliverance ministers had taken ill and was admitted in hospital. His name was Pastor Timi Junior, and he was the youngest and least experienced minister, on the team. There was also the rumor that he was coerced into ministry by his pastor father. After this, Nino felt an occasional nausea now and then. Then Nino got the news that his late wife's family had secured expert testimony that would prove he murdered his wife. Nino knew it was no fluke because her family was one where people hardly ever gave up when in pursuit of a goal. Besides, there were no statutes of limitations to murder—at least not in Cretania. He tried many times to reach his father but to no avail. His world was spiraling downward again and he was getting upset and confused.

Nino thought of calling Mimi but decided otherwise. He realized that he didn't have to contact Mimi. Everyone in church had heard all that was going on in his life. But these problems were a tip of the iceberg. He called Bishop Michael Pockets and discovered even more disconcerting news. The pastor warned him to become prayerful whenever he was not in church for the deliverance program or any other time for the regular meetings. Finally, the pastor gave him the hardest news. Pastor Timi had been discharged from hospital but suffered an attack in his home. Three evil spirits appeared in his living room and warned him stop ministering deliverance to Nino. But the young minister survived the attack refusing to yield to their threats. Nino knew this was coming. He once belonged to the dark world and this was how things worked. No one gets away from darkness without a great battle. He was quite surprised that this resistance hadn't come much earlier. He was glad that Timi was alive and would recover from the bout with illness. The pastor also told Nino not to lose his faith or become afraid as it was all to be expected. The resistance by the kingdom of darkness was now in full gear. "No one leaves the kingdom of darkness for the kingdom of light without a fight by the dark forces. But it will be over soon if we don't give up," Bishop Pockets comforted him. The senior pastor couldn't have said it any better. After the call, Nino comforted himself in the reassuring words of the pastor. But there were more troubles to come.

The next day was the third day to the end of his deliverance and he woke up cheerful and singing hymns. Nino spent all that morning meditating on the Book of Psalms and especially Psalms 18, 91, 118 and 121. There was a voice that spoke to him as he quoted the words of the psalms aloud. "The battle for your soul is on but do not fear for I will be with you always." Nino wrote those words on the wall just behind the left half of the double doors in his bedroom. Those doors opened into the hallway that connected his bedroom to the spiral staircase which led to the hallway on the ground floor. As he finished writing those words he came out of his bedroom and walked down the hallway and went down the spiral staircase to the ground floor hallway. He walked over to the large mirror on the wall on the right side of the main door. With the same felt pen that he had written the words on the bedroom wall he wrote another set of words on the mirror. It was a red-ink felt pen that left a golden streak around the edge of the words it wrote. "I, Nino Strata, have won the war for my salvation. I will not die but live and glorify the Lord." As he finished writing, Nino stared at the words for a few minutes and after he was satisfied he walked back to his bedroom. His plan was to take a few minutes to say his afternoon prayers at about noon. As he got back to the bedroom, he noticed something was different from the way he left the room minutes ago. Nino walked to the center of the bedroom and did a 360-degree turn around the room. As he stared into the large mirror in the wall he saw a strange image.

It was like a vision that hit him with the power of a thunderbolt. In the mirror he could see five figures all dressed in white clothing which shone and produced luminescence that filled the room. Their eyes were red and yellow like fire and they each had a halo above their heads. Nino had seen many evil spirits in his time so he was familiar with evil spirits. But these men were no evil spirits but exuded the kind of overwhelming power that could only be from the God of the highest heavens. He was transfixed to the spot for at least ten minutes as a great feeling of comfort came over him. It was like he was ushered into a whole new world and all his fears had left him.

As he stood there not sure of what to do next, one of the men broke the silence. "Do not be afraid, Nino. We are all on the same side. We are sent to watch over you that you may live and not die. Things are about to get very bloody for everyone in this war especially for you, Mimi and your people. Seek your people and you shall surely find them. Find them because you need them. Be strong and courageous, Nino, for the victory is assured. The Lord will save you from your enemies. He shall kill them all." As suddenly as they appeared they disappeared from the mirror and Nino came out of the trance.

Nino decided not to mention this matter to anyone. He was oblivious of the fact that the greatest attack against his life was near. It was about 9:05 p.m. at the Nino Strata home and the maid, Miss Lena, had just left for the night. Nino usually had his final meal for the day about this time, something he termed the 'night cap.' The maid delivered it to the dining table about five minutes before she left for the night. It was more of a light dessert than anything else, and was made with assorted fruits, salads and sweets with an unsweetened fruit juice to drink. After he finished, he went into the living room to watch both the national and international night news. The news ended about 10.30 p.m. after which he retired to his bedroom. A few minutes later the phone rang, and he walked over to the bed table to answer it. Nino screamed with joy when he discovered it was Mimi. He had not heard from her since the deliverance program began and that was about two days into the program. They talked about general things for a few minutes and then the conversation became spiritual. Mimi informed him that a 'new revelation' had just been received by some of his deliverance ministers. She informed Nino that there was a possibility of holding a night vigil at his home with him in attendance that night. "We may have to be there Nino but I am sorry we don't know why. Just something the Lord has ordered for us. You, I and the ministers must carry out the vigil tonight and tomorrow night. It will start about 12:15 a.m. and run to 3 a.m. in the early morning."

"You still have the key to the house don't you?" Nino replied. "Yes I do, Nino. See you at about midnight, my brother," were Mimi's final words during the call to Nino. "Okay Mimi, see you then," Nino replied before they both hung up the phone. These new developments almost reintroduced worries and fear in Nino, but he dispelled all such emotions. All that had happened gave him great confidence in his faith. Mimi was a good Christian, and she had the second spare set of keys to his home. As he finished his night prayers the large digital clock on the wall overlooking the dressing table was reading 11:35 p.m.

As he lay on the bed to rest for a few minutes before the arrival of his Christian friends, he fell asleep. At once, he found himself facing the picture of images given to him by the strange visitor in the hospital. As he stared with an intense gaze at the picture, he noticed that the there was a central picture on the canvas. He focused all his mental capacity on the picture to discern the central image. And then he noticed it was himself, Mimi and a few others who were on their knees praying. As he looked at his own image, he noticed he was holding the mystery rod in his right hand as he raised both hands towards the heavens. Then he noticed another image on the left, the west side, of the central picture. But he couldn't quite make out this image so he left trying to understand what it was.

As fast as the picture canvas had appeared, it disappeared and another image formed in front of him. There were two sets of figures in front of him and they stood about where the wall was located on the opposite side of the bed. There was a set of figures on his right and another on his left. Both sets of figures had a central figure and many other figures behind those central ones. His instinct told him that this was an attack against him. Nino prepared himself mentally. As he looked at them he realized who they were. It was a visit from the powers he had abandoned when he became a Christian and left the dark world. Nino recognized the one on the right as none other than the strongman of his father's house. His name was

Barzillai, the same spirit that had dominated and determined the affairs in his father's side of the family for many generations. He saw the many evil spirits and witchcraft souls behind him that were under his authority and he almost became afraid. But that was not all because the spirit by his side was none other than Zebulon, king over the legions of the nation of Cretania. Zebulon was much higher than Barzillai but the kingdom of darkness always co-ordinated their activities. And they engaged in co-supervision of projects especially when that project had such a high level of importance. Zebulon had a larger entourage than the strongman and this was just a small fraction of the spirits under him. There were fewer souls with the prince and Nino recognized them all. Nino knew their presence there that night in his dream was not just co-incidence and neither was it just about his conversion to Christianity. He knew there was an important mission, and it had to do with the whole nation. If they failed in their mission to win their target, they must take no prisoners. He had been expecting something like this for a while now. He knew these powers he had turned his back on would never give up on any deserting member, talk less of a senior one like he used to be. Nino had every reason to be afraid but somehow he felt no fear but strength and confidence in his new god. By now, he knew these great powers were by far inferior to Jesus.

"Why have you left us, Nino," were the words of the strongman who spoke first. "You had a beautiful home on this side of the road. You had everything so why leave?" Nino was silent for the first fifteen seconds not sure of what to do or what to say. He knew if he offered the wrong words, tonight may well be his last night on the earth. And it would end in this dream without even waking up to say goodbye to his people and family. He wished to say goodbye especially to his dearest Mimi whom he had known as a friend for only a few months now. But as he thought of Mimi and all she had done for him and all she told him about himself and others, he noticed courage suddenly welling up inside of him. "It was time to cross over to the side of the road that I once belonged. To the side where I have real friends and family who love me and a god that can truly save me even from certain death." Nino spoke up without fear of consequence.

159

"The strength and seal of the House of Strata has always been a black stallion signifying strength and greatness. That will never change in this generation or in many generations to come. So why do you need this change and why now? The time has come for your star to take its place in the history books and corridors of power in this nation, and in the world." Barzillai was now speaking with enthusiasm, but Nino knew there was no love in those words but just the spirit's desire to bring him under his authority and control. It was now clear what they wanted specifically. They wanted him to become a political candidate and hold political office. Nino knew well what these spirits did with people under their authority when those people attained political power. They always used them to destroy as many souls as possible. Even though there were great rewards he didn't want to have blood on his hands. Not any longer and never again. He had once been there. So he gave them a wise reply.

"I have given up the black horse for a white one, sir, and I am never switching back to the old days. I am aware of my destiny and I have chosen to run my race on a white horse. If I win let the light be my glory and even if I lose I shall never return to darkness. My spirit, soul and body are set and determined." Just then there was an interruption.

"Nino, I am the Ruler Lord of Cretania second only to the King of Darkness himself in Cretania. I make laws and have the power over the federal and state halls of power. What can we offer you to return to us and serve us with loyalty as your ancestors? Come back to us and we will someday make you the most powerful man in the country — President of Cretania." It was the voice of Zebulon and he spoke with great authority. As he finished there were echoes of shrills and coos by his subordinate spirits. If Zebulon said it, he could do it because he was that powerful. But Nino was no fool. He knew these powers had seen his star and all that the future held. And he knew they had to know that the Christian God had promised him the same thing Zebulon was promising. That was why they were pleading with him to return to them; because evil powers rarely plead with anyone. As a matter of fact evil powers were the ones who normally have people begging them for favors and material things in exchange for the blood of sacrificial lambs—whether human or animal. But as he thought of replying Zebulon, a voice within him warned him not to look into the eyes of the beast. He obeyed by turning away and starring at the end of the wall in the distant left corner. He couldn't have imagined what was coming next.

"I shall not return to the old ways and I shall visit no coven ever again. I want nothing ever from the old kingdom," Nino answered with even more confidence. And about the same time Zebulon spoke his last words in the conversation. "Your exit has caused so much pain and injury in the kingdom especially in the houses of your father and mother. A great battle for your soul has erupted and the enemy powers are fighting us so hard on your behalf. But you know there will be grave consequences."

As Zebulon finished his sentence Nino noticed two ancient-looking arrows traveling towards him at high speed. Each arrow came from one of the two leaders of the gang of spirits that seemed to have come in peace. But he should have known better. It was not a dream visit but an attack, and all the talk was to use the deception of trying to win him back as excuse for attack. But there was no time now to think. He knew those arrows were the arrows of death if they landed on him or in him. Immediately the arrows left the spirits many of the subordinate spirits disappeared. Nino tried to pursue them or get up and fight as he used to do but he had lost all his witchcraft powers and couldn't even leave his body anymore. He feared the arrow of the principality more because he was more powerful but it didn't matter. Either arrow would kill him if it as much as touched him. He had seen this technique used countless times. Death would be instantaneous and there would be no waking up from sleep. Death would be quick either from heart attack, brain aneurysm, hemorrhage, suffocation, or one or more countless killer medical causes of death. "O Lord, forgive me for the many souls I have done the same harm," Nino prayed silently in his dream.

As the arrows approached him, he could feel their power taking effect on him. In a few seconds he noticed he was suffocating and couldn't breathe. It was like 100 elephants had been placed on his chest. A few more seconds later he felt himself slipping into a coma, and then he saw images of his childhood. His life was flashing before him and he was dying. It was about this time he saw himself in Shiloh General Hospital and there was Mimi by his side. He wanted to tell her how much he loved her and how life in eternity would never be the same without her words and her charming smile.

It was then he heard his name as if someone was standing between him and death and pulling him back to life. "The arrows must have struck by now," he thought. But he heard the voice again, and it was like a powerful but soothing ointment poured on his wounds. The voice called out again and this time he could hear the words even clearer: "Nino, wake up, it's only a dream. Wake up, mighty one, you cannot die. I decree you shall not die but live in Jesus name," Mimi screamed at the top of her voice. At those words Nino opened his eyes as he recovered from the arrows. He couldn't understand why but the two arrows had removed themselves from his body as Mimi spoke those words. "You must take your rod and fight these devils. Nino you are greater than these demon criminals." As she said those words, still screaming, she handed the rod over to Nino placing it in his right hand. Quite dazed and confused by the incidents in the dream, he grabbed the rod and at once he received strength and sat on the bed. He grabbed the rod and he hurled the rod toward the wall where the spirits stood. They stood their ground as if to say, "What could this fool do to us, and with a wooden rod?" But as the rod left Nino's hand it separated along its length into two thick rods equal in dimensions. About the same time the wooden rods had turned into sharp metallic two-edged swords which flew as projectiles with each one flying towards both Zebulon and Barzillai. As they both tried to escape through the wall, the swords seem to have stopped time momentarily because the evil spirits couldn't move. The first edge of the first sword struck the strongman between the sternum and it went deep into the inside of his chest area. All his six eyes showed the pain that he was suffering and from his many mouths and tongues came strange spit. But he had it easier than his fellow. The sword that hit Zebulon went straight for his head. He looked more human than the strongman so his was a much simpler task. The tip of the sword locked in to his head and pierced it between the middle of his eyes. He was a very powerful spirit indeed as his own swords were released to battle the oncoming sword. But Nino's sword found its target, traveling inside the head all the way to the back of the large head. And after that both the strongman and principality vanished together with any remaining members of their entourage.

As Nino woke up fully from sleep, he noticed he was holding the rod in his hand as if he never threw it at the spirits. Mimi was beside herself with excitement and she threw herself at him as he realized that it was all a dream. Besides Mimi was Bishop Pockets standing at the bedroom door entrance. And behind him were the other church members who were there with Mimi to partake in the night vigil with Nino. They all were witnesses to what had just happened and some of them were still praying for Nino. As Mimi held his hands and slowly led him up from the bed, Nino's bloodshot eyes still indicated the ordeal through which he had just gone. "It is OK, Nino. It is well, I promise you," were the gentle words of Mimi as Nino regained himself. Then Bishop Pockets said, "You see everyone, this is why the Lord instructed us to get together tonight to pray. Halleluyah we came on time."

That night the vigil began as soon as Nino was fully recovered from his ordeal. They spent the first thirty minutes thanking the Lord for saving Nino's life. The prayers were silent at times but mostly, about 85% of the time, the prayers were strong and violent. At about 3 a.m., the pastor brought the vigil to an end. By 5 a.m. the church members had all left except for Mimi and her brother, Peter, who spent the night with Nino to comfort and care for him.

As soon as he was feeling a little better, Nino slipped into his inner room at the end of the hidden hallway attached to the walk-in closet. He had taken the excuse that he wanted to change his garments before returning to bed in the early hours of the morning. As he entered the inner room, he walked in haste to the grand clock on the wall next to the entrance door. He removed the clock to reveal the picture from the strange woman where he had hidden it and he studied the many new images that had appeared on the canvas. It was just as he and seen in the dream. The central picture was still the church members surrounding him and they seemed to be praying hard for him. He knelt down in the center, and was also praying with his hands lifted up and the rod in his right hand. But as he went over all the pictures with care, he discovered there was a new image forming in the center. It seemed to be an image of a man wearing a tuxedo and a woman wearing a wedding gown. And in front of them was a minister who was uniting them in holy matrimony. He tried hard to make out the faces of both of the couple getting married but he couldn't. And after a while he tried to identify the minister who was joining the couple. He looked like a familiar face but he could not place the face on anyone he knew. Nino thought aloud to himself who the couple could be. At about that time he glanced at the clock and noticed he had spent over ten minutes in the inner room and Mimi would soon start looking for him. He put the clock back over the picture and hurried through the undetectable metal door that opened into the walk-in closet. As he shut the door behind him, the thought suddenly hit him.

"It can't be possible," he thought to himself. "But what if, just what if, it was Mimi and I? She is my best friend, but wife? No way, it can't be possible. How great that would be if it was so." As he continued to ponder the thought, there was a gentle knock on the closet door. Nino rushed to the door and opened it and sure enough it was Mimi standing there. "Taking plenty of time to change your garments, Mr. Strata? Is there something you are hiding from me?" Mimi asked him smiling. "Oh no Mimi, just taking my time, that's all." Nino gave a quick reply trying to be as discreet as possible. As he came out they both walked through the bedroom and into the hallway on their way downstairs to the living room.

On the next Sunday as Nino arrived in church, Mimi was one of the greeters at the entrance of the church. There was not one mention of what happened during the week. Mimi whispered in his ears as he passed by, "Can we see and talk after the service if it's okay, please?" "Sure I need to talk to you too, Mimi," Nino replied as he smiled at her and then kept on walking. After church they both met at his car and both decided to take a drive to

Nino's home. Mimi told him she felt it was time for both of them to get to know each other better and Nino immediately agreed. As they got into the house, Mimi started on a serious tone in her voice.

"Nino, there's something I need to tell you which I couldn't tell you at the time I received the vision. Yes it is a vision I received so many years ago." "Can I ask what this vision is and is it about me?" Nino asked excitedly. "Yes, I am about to tell you everything. You see, in secondary school while on holiday, my parents called me and told me that the Lord wanted to show me my future. And as you can imagine I was quite excited. That night I saw it all in a vision after my night prayers. What I saw was all I would be and how to get there. I also saw all the people that should be in my life for this great destiny to occur. I am sent to change the destiny of our people Nino, which is this great country of Cretania. But I need only special people in my life to achieve this and I saw the special man that must be by my side to fulfill that destiny." Nino stared at her with great amazement. "If your destiny is to become the president of this country why do you need a man to help you? Do you mean a husband, Mimi?"

"Yes Nino, I need the right husband to do this."
"Mimi, just tell me who this man is and we'll get
him for you whatever the cost to marry you. But
you are so beautiful, Mimi. Which man will not
marry you? He must be a crazy fool." "Nino, the
good news is that I know him 'cos I saw him in my
vision." "Please tell me Mimi, please. No more
suspense." Mimi focused her gaze on him and in a
gentle tone said: "Nino." "What, Mimi? Why do
you keep doing this to me? You keep hiding things
from me just like in secondary school. Why did you
keep this from me all this time? I didn't know how
to tell you how much I love you, Mimi. That is what
happens when you have so much respect for the
one you love."

"I couldn't tell you back then because you
were not a Christian but even back then in
secondary school I knew it had to be you. My
parents counseled me that until you became a
Christian, if ever you did, there was no point telling
you. And that's because you would never fulfill that
destiny as an unbeliever, anyway. If I had told you,
it would have been a joke and then this great
destiny may have been compromised. And you

could have been dead by now. It never would have worked. Don't you understand?" Nino almost couldn't believe his ears and his pent-up love for Mimi totally overwhelmed him. He let it all loose as he had no control over the feelings he had for Mimi Joy ever since their days together as fellow students in secondary school.

"I cannot live without you anymore, Mimi. And now you must marry me, Mimi Joy. Right now, it's time for us to get married," Nino replied, speaking as he went down on his right knee. At the same time he produced a gold ring he always kept in his inner coat pocket in anticipation of this day. Nino could not hold back the flood of emotions any longer. He held and kissed Mimi's hands with great passion as he serenaded her.

"You are the light of my life, the sun in my day, the honey in my tea, the red cherry in my sundae, the engine in my car, the oxygen in my lungs and the air I breathe. MJ, without you I never was and if you reject me, I will never be cos you are the foundation of my empire. You make me complete and you are the joy of my life. You know you are the other half of my destiny and without you, there is no me. I love you too much Mimi so you better kill me before you dare say no."

Mimi threw herself at him as he knelt on the floor, filled with emotion and sobbing as she answered him. "Yes, yes and another yes, I will marry you Nino Strata because God knows I have always loved you. And I will never stop loving you."

CHAPTER SEVEN

A Divine Warning

The great prophet approached from behind the security line where none of the security personnel detected him and no one in the security patrol recognized him. But he was famous among the citizens of the country and popular with the Christian faithful in Cretania. The incumbent president, President Samuel Everlast, knew him only too well. He was same the prophet who warned the president not to marry his current wife Priscilla. Unfortunately, the president ignored him back then since he had committed himself too far into the relationship. And besides that, at that time the marriage guaranteed the union of two of the most powerful houses in the country. It was a union that essentially guaranteed him the presidency of the country. And the guarantee paid off because he was now president and was near the end of his second term in office. It was also the same prophet that warned him not to take the large loan that was then offered by the International Finance Union,

IFU. And that too the president ignored for it was the only way to reduce the rising unemployment in the country in those days, and ensure his election victory for a second term in office. And now he had won both elections despite disobeying the counsel of a man considered as one of the greatest prophets in the country, the president refused to take him serious. For that reason, President Everlast banned all prophets and the like—soothsayers, fortune tellers and seers—from the office and home of the president. But Mr. President, deep down, respected the great prophets too much to put in place any harsh policies or laws against them. Or do the same to the Christians in the country. After all, he was an altar boy in the Catholic Church when he was a youth and the reverend father in that parish took him as his favorite in the whole parish. He would have had a promising career as a priest if he had chosen that path. When he was growing up, at the age of twenty he promised his dying mother he would work hard to one day become a Church Bishop or, even better, Cardinal of Happyness. If he had succeeded, he would have been the first Canadian Cretanian to hold that office. He would also have been the first from his mother's tribe of

Iheni, one of the largest groups of Africans in the state of Happyness. But that was many years ago when his mother was alive. As soon as she died, all religious activity and inspiration to holiness in the family died with her. A few years later their father and his siblings had gone into the dirty politics from which his mother warned them all to abstain. But the House of Everlast ventured into politics and played the game so well that many of them won their various elections. That unprecedented success led to the inception of a great political dynasty — arguably the greatest Cretania would ever know. That dynasty's patriarch and leader was the incumbent's father. And when Samuel became an adult, the mantle of leadership fell on him because he was the first son of his father.

The president's father, Charles Everlast, descended from a long line of men who worked in the transportation of commodities. Two generations before him, Charles' grandfather had migrated to the region from British Columbia in Western Canada. He worked to provide transportation for Cretanian gold bullion and coins to reach global markets. He settled in the Portland area due to its large sea ports but eventually moved to Happyness as the business grew. Over the generations, his sons ran the business until it was the turn of Charles Everlast. It was here in Happyness that Charles met and married the three women who bore him children. The first child he had was when he was two years into managing the business. It was with a beautiful woman with West African ancestry whom he met in the local catholic parish. They named their child Samuel and she raised him, and all her other children, in the Catholic Church. Charles Everlast married two other women after the death of his first wife, Mary, who was the president's mother.

By the time he came of age and the lot fell on him to take over the dynasty there was so much rivalry and bloodshed in the family. So much so that any attempt to get back to religion and faith would just be mockery at best and a death warrant at the worst. The House of Everlast was now deep in the shadow of darkness and he, Samuel Everlast, would neither disappoint his blood nor his calling. He exchanged godliness for political power, reached the pinnacle of worldly power and now there was no going back. He had gotten rid of his conscience to lay hold on the world and its innumerable pleasures. And so, inevitably, he got married to the crown princess of another one of the most powerful dynasties in Cretania—the House of Strongbow. His marriage to Priscilla Lucille Strongbow was not born out of love but out of necessity. It was the necessity to hold on to power and forge new frontiers of power and wealth and the quest for continued dominance of the people. For the Everlast Dynasty, it was more a quest for nobility and then royalty. The plan was to hold on to power so long that the country would essentially become a kingdom. And when the kingdom rises, the hearts of the people would be so full of love for their leader that there would be a smooth transition from democracy to monarchy. And then he would transition from president to king. That was the hidden agenda, the hidden plan.

The prophet's warning on this fateful day was neither the first nor the last. But for this president, the quest for power was irresistible and power was a temptation too hard to resist. The president knew he had made a mortal mistake by turning away from God but he couldn't correct it now. He had gone too far and for too long, and so he resigned himself to praying in secret to the spirit of his mother. He prayed for her spirit to help him and save him from his mistakes and their consequences. She must have been listening and watching over him. Whenever President Everlast was about to make a tragic error, there was always a barrage of warnings from various sources. One of those sources was the prophetic ministry of the prophets of Prophétie.

But this day was different from all the other days the prophet had come to warn the president of impending mistakes he should avoid. It was a gray day, and the president had a nagging headache. The headache began on the previous day, which was Sunday, right after the midday Mass service. As the president stepped out of his car and entered the main entrance that led to his office there was a loud scream at the gate. It was the voice of a man screaming for attention from the president. The president recognized the voice all too well. And the voice was so loud that everyone near the president's office could hear it. The man at the gate kept yelling at the top of his voice, "Mr. President, the Lord, the

God of your mothers has sent me to you. You must listen to him, sir." As the president looked through the waters of the fountain that stood midway between the main entrance and the inner gate he recognized the face. It was Prophet Golan Ezekiel, one of the most famous men in the country and one of Cretania's most powerful and most respected prophets. The security guards at the gate they were taken by surprise to see someone had breached security protocol. The prophet had gained access to the inner gate which was the closest gate to the president's office. But many of the inner guards knew the man at the gate only too well. Just as the security personnel scrambled to apprehend him and get him out of there, the president instructed the chief of his Presidential Guard to let him come in and see him. The chief of guard took the prophet and led him to the president's office. When they were alone, the prophet waited for the president to settle down. After that, the president beckoned the prophet to speak.

"There is trouble in Cretania, Mr. President. And why, don't you know about it?" "What is this trouble, Mr. Golan?" the president replied with a nonchalant tone in his voice. "There is great treason and conspiracy against you, sir. Hands have joined with hands that you might fall. Certain hands that you have fed have joined with hands that fed you to dethrone you, destroy you and all your people," the prophet replied. As the president heard the words "conspiracy," he immediately sat up and was suddenly alert and upset. "But who are they and how do they plan on doing this. Tell me, please. I have an air-tight control over my government and the whole country. So how can anyone overthrow me?"

"Listen, President Everlast, the Lord has given you great power and authority but you have exhibited a trend of disobeying God. But he still wishes to save you and your government seeing you come from a line of God-fearing women. And now the moment of truth is finally upon us. Now if you will repent, be humble and hearken to him this one time he will save you and the people of Cretania too."

The president interrupted him. "What about the people of Cretania? Is this a premeditated genocide or what? They will all hang if they dare carry out their dastardly deed, I swear it." As the president finished speaking, the prophet quickly cut in, "There is no time left now, just listen and obey and all will be well." "Speak prophet, I am listening," was the reply from the president.

"In a fortnight from now there will be a large convention of queer people from all over Yellow River and the world at-large. There shall be many evil people and other enemies of our God whose main goal is to turn this country into hell on earth. Its organizers include your own wife, the First Lady, in anonymity. The Lord of Righteousness has forbidden this convention to take place in this country, for it is part of the plan to destroy righteousness in this country. So, great is the wrath which will come upon this government and this nation that nothing like it has ever taken place in this nation or Yellow River. You must put a stop to it or else there will be disastrous consequences—so terrible that Cretania will shake at its foundations. Yellow River shall turn red with blood and the violence will uproot your government. Then your enemies will put themselves in power." As he finished that statement, Crestar House chief of staff, retired Brigadier General Thomas Ashland, came in to inform the president of an important meeting about to start. He looked at the prophet with disdain and back at the president and gave a tired look on his face as if to say, "Why do you keep listening to these prophets?"

As if on cue, the president got up from his seat and put on his coat to leave and he turned to the prophet as he left. "We shall see next time Prophet Golan when I return from my trip. I shall send for you then. We must find and put down this rebellion in my government, thank you." As he left the prophet spoke his final words to the president. "Mr. President, you must understand that now is the time for salvation. Good day, sir" And with those ominous words, the prophet left the office and was escorted by the guards out of the building. His slim and tall figure moved quickly once he got to the outside of the building. He walked towards the end of the road the building was on and turned into the first street on the right. In no time he reached the end of that street which had presidential guards on both sides. There was a bus station at the bus terminal which doubled as an entrance into the

Crestar House subway. The prophet entered the closest subway door and disappeared into the subway. About 100 meters behind the prophet was a couple dressed in plain clothes that seemed to be tailing the prophet. As they got to the bus terminal, they split to go in separate directions. The man headed in the same direction as the prophet while the lady went into the third door down. They too disappeared into the subway.

As the president's convoy left Crestar House, it began the drive towards the Government Multi-Purpose Conference Center. The center was in the middle of Crestar, the capital of Cretania. As they drove, he began to ponder the words of the prophet. He had ignored the prophets long enough but he couldn't afford to ignore this one. The words were frightening, and it's never been as hard as this before. If this message was true, then for sure he and his government were in big trouble. He knew the other political powers were constantly scheming to be the most powerful dynasties in the land but he never thought they would go this far to sponsor a conspiracy against him. Samuel Everlast had played this game long enough to know that where power is concerned anything goes in the nation of Cretania. "But what about the God factor in all this?" he asked himself. He knew that the God factor was just secondary to the primary cause. All his years in the powerful Pentosi taught him it was possible to achieve anything in Cretania from within that society. It was either by direct influence of the group or indirectly by causing events which will, in due course, lead to achieving their goal. The Pentosi was behind everything evil in this society. Their ultimate goal was to get him out of power and replace him with one of their loyal agents who will carry out all their plans. He had failed to deliver on just one of their secret projects. And also, he made a two-sentence statement about the society and, by Pentosi standards, he had become a traitor. The Pentosi had their hands in every sector of the society and they must have deceived the First Lady into organizing this convention. If a weapon of mass destruction was unleashed at this convention it would lead to massive casualties and his government would get the blame. The people would see it as a punishment by God brought upon the government for their involvement in the many forbidden sins.

Every time there was an attempt to usher in or establish a lifestyle that practiced one of the forbidden sins there had been events that led to mass deaths. It used to be that the forbidden sins were truly forbidden in the great country as the citizenry had zero tolerance for them and any sin at all. The *BSQ*, which was the acronym coined by the Christian believers in Cretania, was a term with which no one, not even businessmen, politicians and the powerful, wanted any association. At least not in public, as that would be tantamount to committing suicide. But, in private, things were so different. The rich and powerful, especially politicians and businesspeople practiced them without any fear of divine retribution. The letter 'B' stood for blood sacrifice of humankind or even animals. This was forbidden for obvious reasons. God hated the shedding of the blood of humankind for whatever reason. And he also hated the shedding of animal blood for the purpose of giving offering to demon-gods, or for abominations like money-making rituals or demonic prosperity. The letter 'S' stood for the practice of Satanism in any form whatsoever. All acts of demon worship, idol making, idol worship and traditional religions were

186

totally forbidden. The most prevalent forms of Satanism in Cretania were witchcraft and occultism. Countless citizens practiced these in secret though speaking on the subjects in public was taboo. But over the past few decades, the occultists had grown bolder and were now venturing public. And finally the 'Q' stood for any queer practice including sodomy, homosexuality, lesbianism and any other similar sexually forbidden lifestyle as embodied in the popular acronym *LGBTQ*.

Gone were the days in which holiness was a term synonymous with this great nation. Those were the days that goodness, kindness and the peace of God were so prevalent in the country. Thus, many good people from all over the world migrated to Cretania. And they settled down and raised families and never left. Prosperity was the order of the day and you were considered to be cursed by God if you were poor or had any long-term infirmity. The same applied if you were in the lowest class of the society or died young. As people came with their ungodly ways, and sometimes their own different gods, they influenced the righteousness of the citizens negatively.

But many things had changed since those good old days. Many decades had passed since the founding of the great country and many good leaders had come and gone. And as sin and evil spread and multiplied, there was a trend of bad leaders coming to power. And then since the days of the great epidemic there was a particularly worrying pattern of wicked ungodly leaders in succession. The current president was not any different but a continuation of that trend. And this president understood what all the current troubles he was going through meant. His government was about to come to an end as there was no way he could persuade his wife to cancel the convention. She was too stubborn to begin with and was a devout lesbian. Priscilla took great pride in being one of the few openly gay first ladies in the world and the only one Cretania had ever known. And, of course, this matter earned her the title of, "The most hated of all first ladies in the history of Cretania." Priscilla Everlast was lost in the spirit of lesbianism and there was no escaping from it. And every passing day she swore by the gods of sex and passion that she would never be ashamed of it but wear it with pride and confidence. She, and others like her, had completely under-estimated the effects which long-term righteousness had on people. Ever since she became the First Lady she encouraged the conversion of straight and not-so-straight people, especially ladies, to the gay and lesbian lifestyle. But many gay people in the closet were now considering coming out but were afraid. They were all terrified but looked up to the First Lady for courage and strength.

The shame and humiliation was too much for President Everlast to bear. His ignorance of his wife's sexual preference until her coming out was even more embarrassing than what he was now experiencing. Of course, the president had often considered all the ways he could get rid of his First Lady one way or another in secrecy. And then maybe he would give an excuse she was ill and so the convention had to be canceled. But then again any attempt to silence his estranged First Lady may prove to be too politically risky. Besides, it may give the Pentosi more ammunition to bring him down faster and with more ruthlessness. If she attended that convention or appeared publicly anywhere near the venue or even worse, gave a speech at the convention, his popularity would drop so low he knew there would be a call by the lawmakers to impeach him. His presidency would practically be over at that point anyhow. He still couldn't get over the fact that his wife's sexual preference had led to the fall of the joint Everlast-Strongbow Dynasty. "What a damned thorn in my flesh Priscilla Strongbow has become, but how can convenience be so terribly inconvenient," he complained to himself. "Of all the things to bring down the most powerful dynasty in today's Cretania, it was a woman, and a lesbian one at that," he cursed out loud. And not one member of the House of Everlast could have foreseen this development. His thoughts began to wander far and wide as he brought his right fist down on his new smart phone that was on his lap. The president was now cursing silently, "Oh my dear Priscilla, my sweet damned Priscilla, to hell with the power, the wealth, and the dynasty. You have caused me too much pain. Yes, you have brought your king too much shame, even ridicule that has pierced his soul. Why should the fate of Anne Boleyn not be upon your damned soul? Priscilla Strongbow, you must die a very painful death and you must die now. You were sent by God to torment me, and my failure to remove you has become my great sorrow. And what about the consequences of this battle on the great Everlast family? Well, the family was dead already by now anyway."

"But how can love of convenience go so wrong and in such a short time. How did this all degenerate so fast? But I know, yes I do. It is my punishment for abandoning the faith and choosing power, lust and the world. But what do I do about that evil poisonous serpent—the Pentosi? How could I ignore that wicked, damned Pentosi? That was where it all began. They gave me a sword too heavy for me to wield and now that I have tried to escape my responsibilities, they plan to get rid of me. No one fails the Pentosi, and I have sent many to their graves in the name of the Pentosi, anyway. Now it's my turn, isn't it? I am the great, everlasting 'Everlast,' the 'King of the Everlasting Dynasty,' and the most powerful man in all Cretania. No, no, no. I am the greatest in the entire Yellow River. Who can kill me? The serpent may bruise my heel but I will crush its head. I will not go down without a great fight because I am not terrified of enemies or even afraid of the damned Pentosi. I will not go down without taking them all with me. When the head falls down, then all fall down."

As he cursed, the president looked at his driver and Chief Security Officer in the front seats seemingly oblivious of what was going on with him at the back. The privacy windows separating the front seats and the passenger area were fully wound up so they hadn't heard a word. And even if they heard or saw him, they wouldn't dare show it or speak a word. Once he was satisfied he hadn't been heard or observed, the president relaxed and leaned back in his white leather seats. He stared blankly at the sun roof of the custom-made bullet-proof Cadillac Brougham presidential stretch limousine. He observed the changing of the color of the sun roof to reflect the change from evening to nighttime. And as he fumed within, he fell into a deep daydream as he recalled the last days he spent together with his wife.

It was many years ago and life at the top had truly taken shape for the first-term president. This particular day was in June and was another one of those manic Mondays. As was the custom of the presidential staff, everyone had the day off early so as to avoid the temptation to overwork. And besides, the drag from the previous day which was Sunday was probably not over as this was the day the president's people loved to schedule their "fun-day" activities. Those who were religious could spend the whole day in church and not be penalized for coming to work late. The party-goers could party into the night and early morning and not show up for work until late morning and they too would not be penalized for it. On this day, the previous day was the Sunday set apart for giving thanks to the God of Cretania for all he had done for the nation and more. Everyone had to be in one church or the other to celebrate "Holy Thanksgiving" which was traditionally marked on the last Sunday of June. On this Monday, the president had sent his staff home at 1 p.m. that afternoon giving them the reason that it was in continuation for the thanksgiving festivities of the previous day. As he arrived back in the residential wing of Crestar House, the presidential mansion, he passed through the water gardens and noticed by a careful unobserved inspection that everything was arranged according to plan. He had sent half of the security of the residential wing home so as to clear the way for his devious plan. As he arrived in the residential living room he sent all the domestic staff home immediately and made certain only the new cook remained at work. In about one hour all the workers were gone except for the cook, and the First Lady who was in her private quarters. His plans were all in perfect motion when he discovered a spoiler—his mother-in-law, the First Lady's mother, had dropped by unexpectedly to say "hi" to the first couple. The president was at first upset that his plan had been ruined but went ahead with the plan anyway. "Two birds for the price of one," he mused to himself, "how splendid." A few minutes later he seated himself in the water gardens and sent for the First Lady and her mother who promptly arrived about five minutes later. The cook served an assortment of newly plucked fruits in three separate bowls. The president's bowl was made of gold while the other two were silver. When the meal was served the two women thanked the president and each one selected a silver bowl and began to eat. The president said the grace after which the two ladies teased him mockingly for being so religious after so many years away from serving in the church. President Everlast smiled as he usually did when he was chided by close friends and relatives but said nothing. In his mind he prayed earnestly that his plan would work and indeed it seemed that his plans were working. While the First Lady's mother ate the fruits speedily, the First Lady was a little bit slow as though she was cautiously trying to figure out something. The president did most of the talking as usual and whatever line of discussion he started he usually ended. A few minutes later, the First Lady tried to offer some of her fruit to her husband to eat but he refused with the excuse that he had eaten his fill already. If the First Lady noticed that he had hardly touched his bowl of fruit she dared not mention if for fear of the consequences. All this time, the president had been keeping a keen eye on both of them as if to make sure they both ate the food in front of them. After about ten minutes of eating the fruit meal, the president got up and excused himself beckoning to the ladies to continue their meal without him.

It was hardly two minutes after the president entered the living room through the balcony that connected the water gardens when Patricia

Strongbow, the mother of the First Lady, collapsed on the lawn of the gardens. As shock gripped the First Lady, she got up and ran to her mother to see what could have happened to the old woman. It was at this point the First Lady herself fell on the lawn of the garden and passed out. Immediately, as if on cue, the new cook appeared from one of the doors of the residential wing. He brought out two syringes from his shirt pocket and rushed to the place where the two women lay unconscious. As he got to the unconscious bodies of the two women, he removed the clip on the syringes and injected each one into the buttocks of both women starting with the First Lady. Immediately after, he carried both ladies one after the other into the residential area of Crestar House. The First Lady was carried to her private room while her mother was taken to the VIP guest room where she was staying. As the cook finished this, the president was already in his second official car. The standby driver who had been waiting all day immediately drove off towards the 'Hidden Gate' of the presidential residence. At the same time the cook backdated the time of the president's exit by one and a half hours.

The president was reported to be attending a church sermon for the welfare and prosperity of Cretania during the one and a half hours that he wasn't in Crestar House. Both ladies had been discovered by the night-shift butler who resumed duty that evening at about 6 p.m. It took three hours for the plan to destroy the two "evil birds" and finally silence them to run its course. It was an excellent plan but not perfect enough. If the president thought he had finally rid himself of two of his worst inside enemies for life, he was just a little mistaken. Patricia Strongbow never woke up from the tragedy and was pronounced dead on arrival at the presidential clinic. But the First Lady survived, howbeit barely, because she had consumed little of the fruits. The fruits seemed to have been bathed in some harmful or poisonous substance. The offensive food or substance was never found, and the story of poison being used was never more than mere speculation and rumor. By the time the ladies got to the clinic on the premises of Crestar House there were no traces of any food poisoning on them or in their bodies. Any and all traces of any harmful substance had disappeared from their blood, organs and body systems. The doctors could only guess at what the substance was from the symptoms they manifested. And moreover the First Lady could remember nothing of the incident except that she was with her mother in the early hours of the morning when they went shopping. Her mother was dead and couldn't recount what had happened to both of them. The new cook was never questioned as the president's office terminated his employment and his whereabouts were never discovered. The president's chief of staff gave the president's alibi as, "Being at a prayer session at the time the incident occurred, an event he went to as soon as he left the office that day and was there for most of the day."

The First Lady was never the same again as the incident had rendered her blind in one eye. She was also partly paralyzed on the right side of her body. The amazing thing was that no one privy to the matter ever suspected the president was in any way connected to these events. And because of the president's great influence, the matter was never made public. His stone had killed one and a half birds, less than the two he targeted but that was still better than nothing by his reckoning. But then the president realized that most of his problems came to an end after this short episode. But he vowed that he would, and he must, try again. He had to finish it before the wounded little bird caused him his presidency and power.

As he recalled these events, President Everlast noticed his motorcade was approaching their destination and he immediately snapped out of his daydream and straightened himself. As he did, he came up with a final plan. His presidency wasn't over yet and he was determined not to step down cheaply or cowardly. But he knew he had to be careful because the most powerful powers in Cretania were at work and they would be watching, and may have even predicted, his every move. He prepared himself for the worst that could happen to him.

But as his convoy arrived at the center for the meeting he had finalized a master plan. He suspected the plan may not keep him in power but will guarantee he gets his revenge upon his enemies. And it will bring him or his family back to power someday sooner or later. As the president's convoy arrived at the closed underground lot that was the front entrance of the building, the car door was opened by a waiting guard.

The president's CSO, Colonel Dani Vale, stepped out to receive the president. As the president prepared to step out, one of the guards stood in the CSO's way as the door stood ajar. The CSO had no reason to suspect any foul play as he thought the guard was new or had forgotten protocol. As the president began to step out of the car, the CSO still had his eyes on the guard just as normal precaution. At this time more of the president's security officers were around the car to shield and protect their commander-in-chief. The CSO had seen enough to become suspicious of the activities going on around the president so he placed his right hand on his pistol. He trained his left hand on the guard while he removed the safety on his gun at the same time. Colonel Dani Vale feared the worst. He had never been wrong before in these kinds of situations but that was just the nature of his training and job. The president had hesitated to come out for whatever reason and that too was quite strange. President Everlast hardly wasted time or delayed in official business. As he tried to remove the guard from in front of him to speak to the president, he noticed the guard reaching into his inner right side towards his gun. With his super-sharp reflexes, Colonel Vale reached for his paddle holster and drew his Glock 19 official gun. As he did this he screamed, "Mr. President get back into the car, we have hostiles."

As the words from the CSO reached the other security officers, sharp reflexes took over. As the primary assailant guard pointed his gun towards the president's head, the driver of the president's car stepped on the gas pedal. This caused the car to move forward by about ten meters. It was this move that saved the president's life; because the first bullet from the guard's gun smashed the rear glass of the president's car. The bullet missed the original target of the president's head. But as the driver brought the car to a stop there was a shot that came out of nowhere which hit the driver and he opened and fled the car while screaming in pain. As the first series of shots went off, there was pandemonium and chaos that broke out in the private parking lot. Colonel Vale, who was the best marksman on the security team, took aim at the primary assailant guard and fired his first shot. The assailant guard was a black belt in jiu-jitsu but his obvious weakness was his less than sharp reflexes.

With one solid 360-degree spinning kick, he had the CSO and the other officers trying to stop him on the ground and temporarily disabled. But before the CSO lost his balance and hit the ground, he fired his first shot. The bullet hit the main would-be assassin in the left shoulder, shattering that shoulder completely. The assailant screamed in pain as his left shoulder joint was blown away to reveal torn flesh and mingled bone. As he tried to fire off another shot towards the president, the deputy CSO fired a shot at the primary guard. As his shot went off there was a strong pair of hands that grabbed the deputy CSO and wrestled his gun from him. The presidential guards had all been oblivious of any other assailants till now. The deputy's shot hit the rear right wheel of the president's car and that wheel exploded with a thunderous bang. That explosion rattled the main assailant guard so that his second and third shots hit the leather seat in the back of the president's car just missing President Everlast's right hip and gluteal region.

The second assailant guard could see that the first assailant guard seemed unable to finish the task so he set out to silence him and then try to kill the president himself. But he was too slow in his task. The first would-be assassin was now badly wounded and bleeding to death. As the second would-be assassin guard tried to shoot the first one so as to prevent his capture, he relaxed his grip on the deputy CSO. That was a terrible mistake on his part. The deputy CSO wriggled free from the secondary assailant's strong grip and fired three shots into his chest. As the shots hit him he fell down writhing in pain but survived as the bullets were stopped by the bulletproof vest he wore. But that fall put him right beside the president's car and in view of the president's back. The president was now down on the seat of the car with his back facing the sunroof of the car. As the first assailant tried to mentally wriggle free of his pain, Dani Vale finally targeted his head and fired one shot at his head. That shot blew the first assailant's head to so many pieces there was blood and brain tissue all over the car and floor. As soon as this happened, the deputy CSO together with the other security officers had their guns trained on the head of the second assailant guard shouting in one accord, "Drop your weapon or you'll die. Drop it or we will shoot." The second assailant started to drop his gun but quickly turned it on his head in an attempt to kill himself. But as he began to move the gun, Colonel Vale's deputy fired his gun at his head killing him at once. In the ensuing confusion, the third assailant escaped from the lot. The other presidential bodyguards went in search of the third, and any other, assailant involved in this attempt on the president's life.

President Everlast was alive and unharmed. As they closed the streets and sealed off the vicinity of the center, the president commanded that the conference must not be canceled. He instructed the CSO to keep the incident as secret as possible so it would not become news. The driver was still alive and rushed to the closest military hospital emergency room. The presidential guards found no other assailants but an investigation was incepted. The federal police executive investigative unit, the presidential guard, and the dreaded military black ops team were all activated discreetly.

The rumors had begun as to what had happened in the parking lot but the security officers quelled them at once. The president's security team increased the security level in the city and the center from Level 5 to Level 9. But the president insisted that the conference must go on. He knew if word got out now about the attempt or if he canceled, then the Pentosi had won the war against him. His plan would never work if any of those things happened. President Everlast swore that would not happen. A few minutes later, the CSO, the Minister of Defense Alistair Cotton, and Chief of Army Staff, Lieutenant General Gyros, were by his side. They had changed the venue of the president's speech from the main podium to the balcony podium. The balcony had a bullet proof glass that stretched from wall to wall which doubled as a transparent TelePrompTer as well. Sixty minutes after the attempt was put down, the conference was ready to proceed.

President Everlast stepped out from the underground parking lot to great applause by the crowds of people awaiting his arrival. As he emerged, he waved to the people and he summoned his chief of staff to walk with him into the building. They entered the executive elevator and took it up to the tenth floor where the conference was taking place. As Mr. President walked into the balcony of the conference hall, the attendees rose to their feet and gave him a standing ovation.

Almost as soon as the president began to make his speech he froze as he looked at the wall on his far right and noticed what was taking place on the wall. A large stroke of fire was writing something on the wall which at first was not legible. But a few seconds later as Mr. President and all the attendees watched transfixed to their seats and positions, the ancient handwriting on the wall was done. As the fires still smoldered on the wall, the writing on the wall became legible and it read:

"I SHALL CAST DOWN THE OLD VINE. I SHALL BUILD A NEW ONE. IT SHALL BE LOYAL TO ME."

CHAPTER EIGHT
Enemy Killer

The Cretanian First Lady sat in the back of the Rolls Royce Stretch limousine with her female companion. Her name was Catarina Aquí and she had been Priscilla's partner ever since they were in university at the University of Barcelona in Barcelona, Spain. While Priscilla studied Business Administration in the School of Business, Catarina studied International Finance in the same school. They met in one of their joint classes together and they hit it off first time. They were partners for two years until Priscilla finished school and returned to Cretania. She had pleaded with Catarina to come home with her so they could live together forever in her home country. With her family connections, she swore to Cat, as she fondly called her, that she would be rich and would receive great care. But Cat refused, giving so many reasons most of which was the fact that Cretania was too religious and intolerant of same-sex relationships. And besides, there were countless stories of the gruesome death that awaited those who practiced forbidden acts like lesbianism. Catarina didn't like Priscilla very much and saw her as a spoiled girl from a rich and powerful family who had no control over her sexual desires. Today she was with one man and the next day it was Cat or another woman. And the next day the same or another man from two days ago and then the next day it would be Cat. And not only that, Priscilla did not, and would never, understand who she really was and why she did what she did for a living. If Priscilla Strongbow ever knew her true identity it would cause an eternal rift in their relationship. But Priscilla was too rich for Catarina to let her go. Catarina had become a mini-millionaire because of her affair with the free-spending Strongbow woman.

After leaving school they promised to keep in touch as they both parted ways. Not long after Priscilla returned to Cretania, she met and began dating the then Governor of the state of Happyness, Samuel Everlast. After a few months of dating, they got married. It was about two years later that he contested and won the presidency and she became First Lady. She had tried to get in touch with Cat but all her attempts failed. And about the last year of her husband's second term in office she got a pleasant surprise. Much to her amazement her main female lover in university showed up in her office. She was the new financial attaché in the Spanish embassy. The First Lady was so overwhelmed with joy and her love for Cat that she did not even bother to verify her story. They resumed their relationship from where they left off so many years ago in university. It was all very secretive so that no one would suspect what was going on, especially the president. Cat feigned sympathy over the incident that cost the First Lady her mother's life and almost cost the First Lady her own life. Because of that incident, Mrs. Strongbow could hardly use her right hand and often walked with a limp on her right side. It was Cat who counseled her and gave her the confidence to put her weight behind the convention in Mystery River. Mrs. Strongbow went one step further—she became the sole organizer of the convention. She footed the bill for everything including the food and drinks, accommodation, video recording, radio and television broadcasting and every other thing. She was even the main reason behind the choice of Mystery River as the convention's venue.

Together, they waited patiently for nine months before the date of the convention. They had traveled to the capital city of Happyness from Crestar by the First Lady's official jet. They landed at Joy International Airport in Joy City and after the First Lady's convoy left the airport they headed northeast towards the city of Mystery River. The First Lady had secretly purchased a small ranch in her mother's name in the cottage country city of Veritas on the outskirts of Mystery River. They arrived in the ranch at 7 p.m. in the evening after a 35 minutes' drive from the airport. After helping with the unpacking of her luggage and those of Cat's, Priscilla asked the bodyguards to leave the cottage. The two ladies spent the next two hours talking about the start of the convention scheduled for the next day. At about 9 p.m., the First Lady suggested they both retired for the night and, at first, Cat agreed. But later in the bedroom Cat decided she would go for a walk and the First Lady thought it would be a good idea. But Priscilla decided she would go to bed early instead.

Cat entered the washroom as though she would take a shower. She turned the shower on to its highest and pretended she was taking a hot bath by moaning quietly as she stepped into the bath tub. She took off all her clothes and threw them on the floor while taking the black coat with her into the tub. She zipped open the right side-pocket on the inside of the coat. There were two lengthy compartments in the pocket. As she opened the first one it revealed a long, slender 18-inch samurai-type sword which was only four inches wide. It had a lock on one end for the insertion and locking of a handle. As Cat opened the second compartment it had a long, slender handle which was about five inches in length. She quickly took the handle and locked it into the sword and cleaned the sword on the back of the coat. As she stepped out of the bath tub, she headed for the bathroom door. On the back of the door was a white night robe which was hanging on the door hanger. She wore the robe and hid the sword on the inside of the right side while still clutching to it. She knew she had to make this quick and silent if she was to succeed. As she opened the door she looked to the left into the bedroom and noticed that Priscilla was falling asleep. But perhaps the First Lady decided to wait for her to finish from the bathroom so as to kiss her before she slept off for the night. As Cat got to the bed, she placed her left hand on her partner's shoulder and whispered into her ears, "God knows I will miss you, Priscilla Strongbow."

The First Lady thought she was referring to the time between her night jog and her returning from it. "I will always be here and you won't be gone so long. Just wake me up when you get back. It should be only kisses and nothing else, of course," the First Lady replied in ignorance of her partner's plan. "I am so sorry and grateful for everything, Priscee. Please forgive me if you can ever," were the words of the penultimate sentence from Cat as she took one final glance at her partner. Cat planted a final kiss on the back of Priscilla's neck. Her mind was made up and as a pro there was no going back. She swore she would make it as memorable as possible.

"A penny for your thoughts, a nickel for your kiss," was the final statement from Catarina just before she produced the sword from under her white robe. The First Lady was just about to turn from her position of sleeping on her stomach to look at her for an explanation of what her last words meant. But she was too late in lifting her head. With one quick strike Cat brought the blade of the sword down on the back of the neck of the First Lady. The force of the blade immediately decapitated her and sent the First Lady's head rolling to the other side of the king-sized bed. Blood gushed out of the open wound shooting in all directions as the former lover scrambled to cover up the bleeding and grab the severed head.

Once she grabbed the head, she placed it in the athletic bag they brought to use for any athletic or outdoor activities. Cat looked at the time and noticed it was 9:30 p.m. and the guards would be expecting her to leave by now and return from her jogging by 10 p.m. She couldn't mess this up as she had only one chance. The contract specifically said that the victim's head must be delivered for the task to be considered successful. She wrapped the head in one of the black nylon bags so that no blood would drip from the bag. If the guards suspected even the slightest foul play, her life would be over.

As she approached the front door of the cottage she began to hear one of the Caucasian Shepherd guard dogs barking loudly. She turned for the last time to look at the body of her former lover on the bed and she almost fainted at what she saw. On the wall above the headrest of the bed the victim's blood had splattered all over. There was a strange writing in blood on the wall that read:

"I AM EL. I KILL ALL WHO HATE ME."

On seeing this Cat was afraid at first but knew she had to be about her business or else it would be end of her life. "What on earth could be going on," she muttered to herself. Cat suspected that the First Lady was killed by one of the many gods of Cretania. "She must have offended very powerful enemies," Cat thought out loud to herself. But the message was so frightening, Cat was afraid she too was about to die. She put this incidence at the back of her mind and continued with the escape plan.

It was only a matter of time before the dogs all joined in the barking so she had to move fast. She kept her cool and stepped outside the door where the two guards looked at her and smiled casually. Then one of them spoke. "I see you are going out for a night jog, Miss Cat." "Yes I am sir, I need it," Cat replied in no hurry. "I hope the First Lady is all OK now," added the second door guard. "Yes she is, sleeping off," Cat replied the second guard.

As she finished, the guards nodded her off and she calmly began to walk in the direction of the ranch gates. As she got to the gate, Cat froze as one of the guards was now leading the barking dog towards the gate and in her direction. Cat knew if she panicked now it was over so she kept her cool. As she looked at the guard post she noticed there were only two guards instead of the usual four that were there when they arrived. The guard holding the dog came close to her and said to her, "Miss, I think we need to search you and the bag. But it may be nothing so no need to worry as it will be over quickly."

As Cat began to put the bag down on the security check table, the second guard rushed to the other guard and informed him that he would handle the search as his colleague had a phone call from the boss in head office. The guard holding the dog immediately handed it to the second guard and ran off to take the call. Immediately he was out of ear shot, the second guard beckoned to Cat, "Miss, you can take your bag and go quickly through the other gate. Go straight on the coconut tree path till you reach the main road. Then you will be OK."

At first, Cat was dumbfounded as she stared at the second guard. He had calmed the dog down somehow and had distracted the curious guard. She couldn't believe that her employers had others working on the inside. "What a night full of great surprises," she smiled calmly. As Cat carried the bag, she hurried towards the third gate and pushed it aside as she began to run down the path between two opposing arrays of coconut trees. She ran for about one full mile before she began to see the main road. From the distance she could make out a black BMW sedan waiting by the side of the road. Cat looked back as she thought she heard dogs chasing her and their barks getting louder and closer. Her attention was caught by the figure in the driver's seat that wound down its glass and shouted quietly for her to hurry up into the car. As she arrived at the car, the back door behind the driver's seat opened up and she jumped into the back seat. She had never been so relieved in her life as when the car drove off and disappeared down the road and into the night.

****

A few days had passed since the vicious attack on his life by the most powerful demons in the kingdom of Cretania. And Nino Strata was not ready to stand by and let evil destroy him. He had taken the initiative in this war and he was determined to take the battle to the enemy. They wanted him dead so badly they were now throwing everything at him. But he vowed that he would kill them first before they got to him. It was all about who got to who first, anyway. After consulting with Mimi, he decided he would find out the real details of this war. They knew it was a battle for the soul of the country and it was to preserve the light from destruction by the powers of darkness. But what was the deep story of the whole matter? Nino had learned from his years in the dark society that to succeed in anything you must work from the deep and innermost parts of the matter. He knew that the deeper you went, the better your chances of success. And then after discovering what the depth of the matter was, it would be wise to know the identities of all his enemies. On the wall of the inner room, he posted large notes and started research he hoped would one day give his side an advantage in the war. Nino would begin by gathering information— the best place any true warrior should begin. He subdivided the wall into three sections with each section having a different heading. Then he labeled the first section 'My People,' while the second section had the label 'My Enemies.' Nino recalled the words of the man in the mirror: "Seek your people and you will find them. Find them because you will need them."

The third section was the most elaborate of them all and he had it on the wall opposite the curious picture. He labeled this third one 'Success Strategies.' He realized that most, perhaps all, of the information that came into this section would be directly from the images of the picture.

Nino made entries into the first section one name after another. Mimi Joy was naturally the first name while his father's name was next. He added a few names of those who had proven themselves to be friends over the past few months and years. When he got to the second section, he entered names of his enemies. The first name was the Legion King of Cretania and the second was the chief demon of his father's house, Barzillai. He then wrote the names of all the demons he knew would be in this war and surely not on his side. Those names included the chief demons of the Houses of Nestel, Spitzum and all the other houses he was connected to in one way or another. Then there were the other enemy demons he knew. As he wrote these names, he realized he had made a great error of judgment. He just realized that the first few names on the enemy list were all evil spirits. But he seemed to have omitted the greatest spirits who were friends and should be on that list. He quickly rushed to the friends list and rearranged the names. The first name was now 'El' and the next were the five men who appeared in the mirror. And then there was the strange 'picture woman' in the hospital who brought him the picture. After he added them to the list, he then added the names of his human friends. At this point he understood what the hierarchy should be on any of the lists he made.

First, it should be the names of spirit beings and other supernatural beings. Then there must be supernatural objects like the picture. And finally, there should be the names of humankind who were fellow combatants in the war. Nino believed these three categories in the two lists should produce a true picture of the participant list in the war. As he strove to create the perfect lists of enemies and friends, a great temptation came over him. Every time he tried to figure out if a suspected friend or enemy was fit for the list, his eyes would fall on the great picture. And as his eyes caught the picture, he would fixate on its blank canvas for a long time before turning back to the lists on the wall. Finally, after about the tenth time of the pictorial distractions, he couldn't resist the temptation any longer. He decided he would make use of the picture for a few minutes or maybe an hour. Those few minutes would become almost an eternity in that room.

After about one hour using the picture a great idea occurred to Nino. He needed to give a name to the great picture for the sake of discretion amongst other things. So he named it 'Vignette' and wrote that name on the wall just above its upper frame. Throughout this time of using the picture and querying it for friends and enemies, it was business as usual as Vignette one again proved its invaluable worth. One after the other, the picture had produced images in the east, north and south. The names of enemies appeared in the north and east sections while his people and friends showed up in the south and east portions of the vignette. Nino was pleasantly surprised at the volume of intelligence this one picture had provided him and he now could see how this battle had been won already. There was the vignette, the rod, the people, not to mention the heavenly power and visitors, who would join to fight this war.

"There was no way the people of the light could be defeated in this war," Nino reassured himself. But just as he celebrated a future victory, an image began appearing in the center of the vignette. It was the much-dreaded central image which meant there was something urgent or a potential danger that was lurking somewhere. As he focused on the central part, he could make out a familiar face which seemed to be someone close to him or in his family. A few seconds later, the image was fully formed, and it was now clear and well-focused. The identity of the image shocked him as he didn't know what to make of this image that had just formed. If this image was shocking what was to appear next would terrify and dumbfound Mr. Strata. Before his two eyes, the young woman he knew so well began transforming into someone else. As he continued to look, she was slowly turning into the wicked Aunt Melina, his mother Maraya's age-defying aunt. "But how could this happen," Nino screamed out loud to himself as the countless implications of this revelation dawned on him.

"O my dear mother, how could we all not have seen this evil?" Nino began crying, at first silently. He slowly sank to the ground to support himself as he had grown too weak to stand on his feet.

"I am so sorry, Mona, I am so, so sorry. I failed you so terribly. You warned me but I won't listen. Please forgive me." Nino was now crying aloud but good for him the inner room was sound proof and no sound was heard outside the room or the house. He was in such an emotional state that he did not notice the new images forming in the central, northern and southern portions of the canvas. The inner room was not only sound-proof it was also entry-proof meaning that no soul or spirit could enter inside from outside the room. Only the reverse movement was possible and no demon, witch, wizard or evil object could enter to harm anyone in the room. The heavenly visitors had seen to implementing this spiritual technology once they arrived here. But even though the room was entry-proof to the spirit realm, it was not entry-proof to the power of mind control. The enemy waiting on the outside not only came with a large and powerful contingent but also had the power to control minds from near and far.

As Nino continued to cry seated on the floor, he instinctively looked up at the picture canvas and noticed the new images. He froze and his tears cleared away at once. The enemy was at the door and this was no time for tears or emotions. He jumped to his feet as he noticed a strange power trying to crush his head. It felt like a strange, powerful force was trying to squash his head between the palms of its hands. He knew he had to act quickly or else he could lose his head after it had been crushed to pulp. He thought about the Nino of the past and what he would have done. If he hadn't lost his powers to leave his body and fly, he would have done just that and gone out to confront and kill this assailant. But that was all in the past and he couldn't do those things anymore. As he pondered what to do in this emergency, he looked at Vignette for answers. It was then he saw what he was looking for in the central image. Three new images had appeared in the north and south of the canvas. In the south there was the rod, and a fiery shining sword. The northern image was Melina with two unknown persons who looked like men. In the heat of the moment, Nino knew exactly what the images were telling him. He ran as fast as he could to the rod on the table beside the vignette. As he grabbed the rod, it turned into a red-hot glittering sword. Once he held the handle of the sword, his eyes were open and he noticed he could see through the room into the spirit world.

As he looked outside the room, he saw the soul of Melina with two of her colleagues. The heavenly friends had contained the other members of the contingent but these three had somehow made it to the hall outside the inner room. Nino moved fast like any true warrior should and went straight for the part of the room where Melina stood on the other side of the wall. He was starting to become dizzy because of the crushing grip on his head. With one strike, he thrust the sword through the wall to the other side and into the never-aging Melina. As soon as the sword entered her, the tip came out through her back and she slumped to the ground. The two souls by her side disappeared at once. After a few seconds on the floor, the lifeless soul of Melina also disappeared. At once, the grip on his head ended. As Nino moved back into the room, he noticed all the evil contingent were gone and there was so much blood dripping from the sword. He laid the sword on the ground in front of Vignette and bowed his head down to the ground. Nino gave thanks and praise to his God all that night and into the early hours of the morning. After that, he tried to call Mimi and inform her of what just happened but his instincts of secrecy and discretion decided otherwise. "She would find out if she doesn't know it already, anyway," Nino convinced himself.

One day later, he went back to the room to the spot he dropped the sword. Nino found that the blood which dripped from the sword was still there on the floor. The blood was as real as blood from any physical encounter. Later he left the room and went outside the hall to the spot where Melina and her colleagues had stood. Here, he noticed not one but three spots of blood. Nino didn't try to understand what had happened. He just ordered for a maid cleaning service to come and clean up the house. He had only one joy in his heart and that was that he had gotten some vengeance for his mother and his wife. And not only that, he had now taken one life, maybe three lives, in this war which had now become so real to him. His innocence in the matter had now officially come to an end. He took the rod, which had now transformed back from the sword, and held it up high and spoke to it. "I will give you a name now you mighty sword of El, the great enemy killer. As from now on you are 'Yerevel,' the great awesome destroyer."

CHAPTER NINE
Death by Arrow

The congregation of the Assemblée Prophétique de Dieu was a small one as compared to the traditionally large churches in many other states. There were well-known large churches in Shiloh, Happyness, Calazar and Western River which formed the largest Christian assemblies in the country. But in Prophétie, which was well-known as the home of the prophets, the churches were usually small to medium in size. And this was one reason the servants of God in the state boasted about being the believers closest to God in the country. It was believed that the fewer the number of believers in a ministry, the more effective would be that ministry's service to God. But on this day there was so much to talk about and the few numbers of the various ministries' members was neither on the agenda nor was it up for discussion. These were the days of thunder and lightning, loud and dark rumblings in the heavens, the powers of light versus the powers of darkness. The attacks from the dark side against the people of light were coming at an alarming and furious pace. It had become necessary to step up the battle against the darkness if the people of light wished to survive the attacks. The forces of darkness were in a desperate hunt for the soul of the Cretanian nation and they were leaving no stone unturned. But the great prophets whose grandfathers founded the nation as a Christian nation were now all aged. They were the third generation of those great, powerful and fearless Christians. Many of the prophets did not have successors to hand over the baton of their great legacies. And for many of those who had successors, those successors lacked the power and zeal of God, traits that had been the hallmark of past generation of prophets.

The community of Christians in the state of Prophétie had been gathering in this church faithfully for the past three weeks. They planned to talk about the events currently taking place in the country. As it was on the previous night and every night for the past seven days, the first to speak to the congregation was the prophet, Gabriel Nautilus. And then there would be other speakers, and then hymns, praise and then the prayer sessions after which the meeting would close. Nautilus' grandfather was one of the founders of this church together with the likes of Théo Lucas and Noah Timothée who were all revered as great prophets in their days. His father, the legendary Eliyahu 'Le feu de Dieu' Nautilus, was one of the greatest prophets of his own generation. As the opening prayer ended, the host invited prophet Nautilus to take the pulpit.

The man called Nautilus was a slim, medium-sized man with a perpetual smile on his face. He descended from multiracial heritage and, besides his citizenship of Cretania, had ancestors from three different nations. Two of these nations were France and Germany while the third was the nation of Quintos in northern Yellow River. His immediate ancestors met in Cretania and his fathers were considered highly reputable prophets in the state of Prophétie. Prophet Gabriel Nautilus stood about 5 feet 11 inches, slightly bald with a strong French-Cretani accent. He was one of the most revered prophets in Cretania. As he got to the pulpit he began to speak into the microphone.

"My dear fathers, mothers, sons and daughters and children in the fellowship of our God, Jesus, I greet you welcome. Today marks the fortieth year of the end of the great scourge and epidemic called Sepsis. It was an unfortunate time and one which claimed many of our good people. But the powers that unleashed that wicked tragedy upon this country are not finished. No they are not done. They are now calling for the soul of the country altogether and not just the flesh and blood. They plan to take over the whole country and put us, the good people, in perpetual bondage. But that will never happen." As he uttered these words, there was uproar of approval and then applause. The great prophet waited for the applause to subside before continuing.

"We need to fight them with the only power we have and we shall overcome. At last, a few days ago I had a revelation on how to defeat them. Our Lord will always fight the battles of his people and this case is no different from any other one. So, hear what the Lord has done to defeat the great enemy-spirit Zebulon and his forces. In the city of Shiloh a child was born, a great warrior who shall rise to become the sword of the highest god, El, against his enemies. A great stallion, he shall overtake his enemies, uproot the evil tree from the roots and devour them in fire." As he finished, the prophet translated his words to French by himself.

As the great prophet finished, he went on his knees and bowed down on the floor in front of the large sculpture of Jesus as he hung crucified on the cross. He got up after about five minutes on the ground. Immediately he stepped down, the minister who was making the introductions got up and quickly walked up to the secondary pulpit to announce the next speaker. His name was Apostle Jean-Baptiste 'JB' Joseph, who was also popular in the local religious community, but not so much in the country. He got up and approached the pulpit as he heard his name called by the man making the announcements. As Apostle Joseph got onto the stage and took the pulpit, he sang some of the favorite songs in that church. As soon as he finished the praise worship, he led the congregation in prayers. After the prayers, he too began to condemn what the devil and his servants in Cretania were doing to destroy the country and its people. He closed by informing the people of what the Lord had showed him.

"People of Cretania listen to what our God has done for this great nation he founded by himself. He has given the word for all the enemies who have aligned themselves with Satan and the King of Cretania to perish with immediate effect. To achieve this goal he will send his servants and they will fight this battle with his power and the battle will be over in this generation after the wicked queen dies." The apostle paused for a few minutes and then continued. "I had a vision by night and in this vision there was an army of warrior soldier ants who gathered around one young great ant to strengthen and empower him. This little ant went to battle against the great queen and her armies. He was given bow and arrow and fire with which to stalk and kill the enemy. He shall vanquish all his enemies."

As he finished his statements, the announcer called upon the third and final speaker, the great prophet Golan Léo Ezekiel. The prophet quickly came up to the pulpit and began to minister to the congregation. He wasted no time in getting down to the business of the day.

"I had a dream, actually a nightmare my friends, and I saw a bee and with her there were many other bees. And this one bee was favored even from birth for she is the daughter of a great king. And as I looked a great hand came and strengthened this small bee that it became a great bee. It came to a foreign land and started its own hive and became the queen amassing great powers and wealth. And when she became great she became a great thorn in the sides of the original bees of the place where she made her hive. She will come in by great words and wisdom and when she has power she turned the hive into her own kingdom. She will seduce many with her great beauty and destroy many with her wicked power for great was her power. I saw she had no regard for the Most High and she afflicted the people of the cross seeking to destroy the light and remove it from the land. But she will finally be defeated by the great sword, by arrow and by fire. She will be strong indeed, and cast her enemies down tolerating no enmity in her great kingdom. Her power is her father's kingdom, charisma and her beautiful parts. She is the punishment for the sins of the people and that was the door they used to enter the great hive. Our sins have become a terrible snare unto us and destroyed the great covenants that our ancestors made with God."

The prophet paused for a while to roam all over the sanctuary with his eyes. Then he raised his voice unexpectedly screaming, "The cup of sin of Cretania, the great Cretania, is full and overflowing. And it has been overflowing for many decades now. Now the devil seeks the soul of Cretania, you and me and everyone else. And now the power and hour of darkness are upon us." And then he paused again for about ten seconds and continued with a solemn, melancholic tone.

"My people, there is great evil now come to Cretania, a terrible storm rushing towards and encircling us like a deadly cold whirlwind. I pray we shall still be standing when we reach the end of the storm. I pray we will repent and return to our good and kind God so he can be our Lord once again." He ended the speech and immediately left the pulpit through the back door followed closely behind by his ministry staff.

The translating minister mounted the pulpit and translated the words of the last two prophets to French. As soon as the translating minister finished his translations, he added a few final words of his own in French.

"Mes chers amis, frères et sœurs, écoutez bien. Nous savons qu'il y a des temps difficiles, mais je sais que nous devons enfin vaincre. Les batailles peuvent être difficiles et il peut y avoir des blessures. Mais nous devons durer jusqu'à la fin. Et si c'est le destin que nous devons mourir, alors nous mourrons et nous allons au paradis. Merci beaucoup."

A few minutes later, the host minister had rounded up the meeting and the congregation left for the day.

****

In the city of Goldport in the middle-eastern state of Portland, Miss Esther Strongbow strolled gallantly into the store of 'Uptrend Fashions,' which was the biggest fashion store in the state. Her two bodyguards, one male and one female, went ahead and behind her as usual in all the places she visited. She was pretty, mixed race, in her late-twenties and stood about 5 feet 9.5 inches weighing about 150 pounds. She was the least famous of the Strongbow women and that was probably because she was the youngest daughter of JG Strongbow who was the patriarch of the Strongbow Dynasty. She was also quite shy and a total bookworm. Esther believed in the mantra that, "The amount of skill you have determines how high you rise in life regardless of family background, nationality or tribal origins." Her mother had taught her the importance of intellectual achievements, wisdom and the fear of God Almighty; and the absolute importance of belonging to Jesus throughout life. During her school days, Esther and her mother, Caryn, had discovered that she was gifted in the areas of finance, economics and maths. That was what informed her choice of a major in economics in the university and eventually attaining a doctorate degree in the field of economics. Just five years after bagging her Ph.D. in economics from Goldport University, which had the best economics department in the country, she had invented many brilliant economic theories and products. But she was not one to blow her trumpets. Besides, her inventions were being marketed under the family's financial corporation, Strongbow Financial Company. But it was not just her brilliance that made her so successful in life. It was also because of the fact that she had a secret talent which had saved her life countless times. This secret gift had saved her not only from her enemies in the family but also the many enemies of her family and herself outside the family. She was the only one who knew this secret. Not even her mother, who was closest to her, knew her secret. Many family members had been lost due to the incessant attack of external and internal enemies. Though they loved to believe that they had no enemies on the inside the truth was far from it. But Esther knew all their internal enemies for one main reason—they had all attacked her or tried to harm her at one time or the other. She may have been the youngest in the family but Esther was the strongest intellectually and spiritually. And there were few in the family who didn't know this fact. This information had caused her so much trouble in her young life. She had been trained by her mother, who knew her youngest daughter's great star, to survive the wickedness of this world. And that training had saved her on countless occasions. There had been many attacks against her both physical and spiritual, with most of them being spiritual and occurring in her dreams. There had even been two attempts each on her life in the physical and in the spiritual. She knew how great she would be but she had only been informed that her destiny was only about the Strongbow family. Her mother had informed her on many occasions that she would one day be in control of the whole family. She couldn't have imagined how important her star was and the kinds of enemies that were watching and targeting her because of that star. Her enemies wanted her dead, and she was still quite ignorant about the reasons. But she comforted herself that come what may she was ready for them and for whatever they planned against her.

Wherever she went she was always ready for whatever adversity came against her whether spiritual or physical. She had suffered so much in her young life and she was now used to warfare, especially spiritual warfare. This hot June day in 2005 would not differ from the others. As she made her choice of designer clothes, shoes and watches, two men each wearing colored hoods—one red and the other blue—entered the store. The two men wore black T-shirts and blue jeans with blue snickers and entered the store without being noticed by any of her bodyguards. Within a few minutes both hoods had positioned themselves on the two sides of Miss Strongbow and her bodyguards. They were pretending to be checking out merchandise before buying them. Esther's bodyguards carried the Colt M1911 automatic pistol for firearms. The red hood was by the female guard while the blue hood was by the male guard. On cue, the two hooded men each brought out a gun, both Glock 21, and pointed them at the male and female bodyguards respectively. Each one of the hooded men fired three to four shots at the same time. The male guard was hit in the right side of his face and went down at once. Esther's female bodyguard had sharper reflexes and she turned to see the man closer to her as he was producing his weapon. She acted fast to remove her client from danger and then tried to protect herself. She pushed Esther into one of the changing rooms nearby. Then the female bodyguard grabbed a large bag sitting nearby that she may protect herself from the gunfire. One of the shots fired at her hit her in the breast close to her left nipple and she yelled out a curse as she fell to the ground. The female guard produced her gun as fast as she could to shoot back at her shooter. As she took aim, the red hood fired another shot but this time it missed her head slightly. The red hood then fired yet another shot but this time it struck the female guard on the side of the neck wounding her and almost severing her jugular blood vessels. But before the red hood could fire another shot, the female bodyguard had fired one bullet at point-blank range at his chest. And the bullet hit him entering near his heart wounding him fatally but not before he fired his final shot. A few seconds later both the female bodyguard and the red hood lay on the floor lifeless.

As all this was going on, the blue hood had gone in search of the body of the male bodyguard to make certain he was dead, and if not to finish him off. He was over-confident as he believed the head shot had killed, or at least incapacitated, Esther's male bodyguard. It was a big mistake on his part as the male bodyguard was still drawing breath and was not dead. As the blue hood came into view, the male guard fired two shots with his last strength at the groin of the blue-hooded assailant. One of the bullets hit him on the right groin area severing the femoral blood vessels on the right side. But the blue hood was able to fire off one more shot to the temple of the male guard before falling to the ground yelling in terrible pain. This last shot was a perfect hit and it shattered the head of the male bodyguard.

At this time the mall police had entered the fashion store and were evacuating the surrounding area. They approached the scene of the shooting with their semi-automatic pistols drawn and ready to shoot. As the blue hood hit the ground, he realized that he had to get to the changing rooms to look for and kill Esther Strongbow. But he realized he could only crawl due to his gunshot wounds; and he knew he had a short time before he bled to death. As he approached the changing room where he hoped to find Esther, he noticed the door was shut tight. He assumed his target was behind the door and she was trying to protect herself by locking herself in the room. On the inside, there was Esther Strongbow who was saying a quiet prayer for God to send help to save her. As soon as she finished praying to her God, she turned bravely to face the door despite the imminent danger. She raised her hands and placed them on the door. As she closed her eyes, she began to utter silent words like she had done so many times before in similar situations.

"Fire, oh fire, from the fiery lake of death,
Hearken now to my words, fulfill my desire,
Arise and fall grievously by your great fury,
Upon all, who would my dear soul expire."

As she prayed, a fire began close to the changing rooms which formed a barrier hindering the blue hood from getting to her. It was then she noticed a sound behind her and she realized a door was opening behind her. Esther was shocked because she had not noticed any door behind her when she entered. As she slowly turned, she thought it was a third assassin. But she knew that her gift had never before failed her. So, she quietly resigned herself to the terrible fate she thought awaited her.

As she looked back, she saw two men dressed in the same white flowing linen garments which she had just seen on sale in the men's clothing section in the store. Immediately their eyes met, the man on her right spoke first. "Do not be afraid, Esther, we have come to save you. Come with us or you will die." But Esther was too afraid as she had never before been saved in this way. As the two men saw the frightened look on her face, the second man who was on her left spoke to her. "The assailant would be here soon and even if he misses, the police are here and some of them may be enemies of your father and family. You must leave this place at once." As he finished speaking the blue hood was at the door and fired a shot to destroy the door handle so he could get into the room. As the shot took out the handle, Esther looked at the men in horror and was about to say something. But the men held her by the hand and took her with them disappearing through the wall and appearing in a large field. As they entered the field, the man on the right told her that place was one of her family's hidden properties in Portland and that she would be safe there. Esther quickly recognized the field as part of a private farm owned by her father which he had given to her mother in his will. The two men left soon after they arrived on the farm. But before they did they warned her not to leave the farm for at least three days, and never to talk about the matter to anyone.

Back at the fashion store, the fire had engulfed the store burning down much of the store. The police eventually filed their report which said the fire was responsible for killing the blue-hooded shooter and others who perished in the store.

****

The city of Summit, the capital of Calazar, was the home base of the family of the Grinders. The patriarch of the family was the 'Old Horse'

Lukas Grinder. He earned his reputation by being one of the most ruthless and fearsome soldiers that the nation had ever known. If there was one thing the House of Grinder loved to pride itself on it was that they were generations of soldiers and were natural soldiers for that matter. They descended from a generation of men and women who wore military uniforms virtually all their lives. Joseph Grinder was the grandfather of Lukas and he was the first Chief of Army Staff of Cretania. This was about the time the country had been founded when the missionaries, regional leaders and the industrialists joined forces to create the country. Joseph had three children, two sons and one girl, of whom the eldest was Lukas Grinder. Lukas Grinder had one son and many daughters. The son was the youngest and he called him Lukas Grinder II. Lukas Grinder Senior entered the army through military school after graduating as second lieutenant. His father's position helped him to rise through the ranks fast and he made colonel in just ten years. He rose to become general, and also Commander of the Presidential Guard under three presidents. With such a distinguished military service, Junior quickly followed in his father's footsteps. When Junior turned colonel he was already one of deputies to the Chief of Army Staff. By the time he turned full general he was promoted to the highest office a serving soldier could hold in Cretania—Chief of Defense Staff. The House of Grinder was now one of the most powerful in Calazar. But beside their natural flair for hardness, they were also known for their womanizing. Their love for women was the only thing that would ever get a Grinder into trouble with anyone or anything because they were hopeless womanizers. It was this uncontrollable desire for women that earned Lukas Grinder II his nickname. And every generation passed down to the next one a more virulent strain of the womanizing disease. Without any doubt it was a family disease, and a destructive one for that matter. By the time he turned general, Lukas Grinder II had slept with so many women in Cretania that he had made so many enemies. Some of the women were the wives, concubines or lovers of his subordinate soldiers, other subordinates or other people. But that was nothing new as it was a custom in the family line and every generation was guilty as charged. But this trait would cost General Lukas Grinder II dearly. The general had an affair with a woman married to a junior soldier and she got pregnant with his child. In the grand style of King David of Israel, he had the junior soldier, a sergeant, killed in a drive by shooting that was made to look like an accident. Unfortunately, the truth came out and General Lukas Grinder II was court-martialed and removed from the CODS office.

But that was the beginning of his troubles as many women now came forward with paternity claims stating the general was the father of their children. The general was never married, and it was estimated that as many as seventeen children had been born to him by various women all over Cretania. Other sources put the number of children born to him at twenty-one and the number of mothers at ten. One of those children was given the name Jacob and his mother's name was Lily. Lily was the daughter of one of the most powerful men in Cretania in his day—Charles Everlast—the father of the incumbent president. His affair with Lily Everlast began when he was a second lieutenant just out of military academy. And by the time he was promoted from the rank of Major to the rank of Lieutenant Colonel she had their first child and they named him Jacob after the biblical character for his wisdom and cunning. To save his children from the shame he brought upon himself, Lukas Grinder II sent the most promising ones abroad and enrolled them in military academies. This was done only with those children he believed had military potential or had great future potential otherwise. One of those children was Jacob who was enrolled in the local army, registered for foreign training and sent to the United States for military training in their military academy. But in all this, no one knew where the Grinder children really were because if there was one virtue the family had it was the ability of doing things in stealth mode. Lily had become wise to know that life was full of trouble and to escape and survive it was absolutely necessary to become a Christian. She had joined one of the Full Gospel churches at the invitation of the gynecologist who delivered her. This was about the time Jacob was born when Lily almost died giving birth to him. She swore she would never have another child but Lukas presided over her to have one more, and if possible a girl. Two years later they had twin girls, Cherry and Rosy. Ever since she became a Christian, she brought up all her children in the church, teaching them to always follow righteousness. She had all her children's habits in order except for Jacob's love for women which sometimes led to his womanizing.

But as most of the Grinder children were entering their twenties and thirties it was discovered by the Grinder mistresses that Lukas had appointed Jacob as his successor and sole heir of his estate. This was no surprise because it was no secret that Jacob was the favorite child and son of General Lukas Grinder II. This matter caused no small uproar in the family, and all hell was let loose in the family. It took the writing of a new will by the general for the mothers of his children to be appeased. But not all of them were appeased. The mothers of the two youngest boys hatched a plan to deceive and defraud the general and take over the estate at the death of the general. The second to the youngest son was named Jumbo Grinder by his mother and he was hardly ever seen by his father. In fact, Lukas Grinder had seen his two youngest sons just five times meaning that he barely knew them or their mothers. He only saw them when the other concubines were not available to live with him. Jumbo's mother, Jacklyn, who was rumored to be a high-class escort changed her son's name to Jacob James Grinder II. All his documents, including birth certificates, had been forged in that name to match the data on the records of the real Jacob as his father. These documents were back-dated by seventeen years as if Jumbo had been born by the real Jacob Grinder. When the general died all they had to do was show proof that Jacob was dead and he had a son before he left to school in a foreign country. It was a well-laid plan as Jumbo was actually fifteen years younger than Jacob and they both had a striking resemblance to their father. This made it possible to pass Jumbo as Jacob's real son. Supposedly, Jacob was in the neighboring nation of Atlantis in the military academy there. And to secure the proof of death, the accomplice mistress, Amara, was scheduled to travel to see Jacob with an important message from his father. She was familiar with Jacob as they had lived together in the same house when he had just graduated from high school and was waiting to leave the country. And supposedly, both Jacob and Amara once had a brief affair which neither of them ever talked about since then. Jacklyn had arranged a meeting with the general who was now in his seventies and advanced in age. "I will give him the best sex he ever had and I will kill him, Amara, I swear it by my god, Baalim," Jacklyn had boasted to Amara. Even at his old age, Lukas Grinder was still a sucker for beautiful well-built women and he agreed to meet with Jacklyn. Once the general and Jacob—who was the sole heir—were dead, Jumbo would inherit the great Grinder name and fortune. That was the plan. But even the most brilliant plans have the habit of failing woefully. And this plan was fool's paradise compared to what was about to take place.

On a warm summer day in July in the year he truly turned 17, Jumbo Grinder was on the beach of Grinder's Bay. This beach was named after his great-grandfather Joseph Grinder. It was the day of the New Moon festival and carnival in the state of Calazar. As he moved from one group to another on the beach to socialize and greet friends he focused on a young woman who had been smiling at him all afternoon and evening. He sent his bodyguard to invite her over to his table and she promptly agreed and followed him to the fake Jacob Grinder. He introduced himself as Jacob Grinder and she introduced herself as Sandy Dean. She then explained to him that she was a university student who had come a long way just to achieve one goal; and once she fulfilled her goal she would quickly return whence she came. All his attempts to find out more about her proved futile, so he gave up on his attempts. She boasted to him that if she achieved her goal, she would become like a queen in her clan.

"I expected the firstborn son of the 'Old Horse' to be a little older and more mature," Sandy chided him as they continued with their conversation. "I believe in youth, Sandy, and I use tens of beauty products to keep me clean. If you know wha' I mean darlin'." He replied her in his usual boyish charm and accent.

"I guess I do, Jacob. How is your father? I heard he hasn't been feeling well lately." She asked him to see if he was really Jacob Grinder as she had some doubts judging from his youthful looks. She knew the Grinder men were hopeless womanizers, and she expected they would always try to look young and boyish just like their father. But as she continued to size him up, she noticed his striking resemblance to General Lukas Grinder II especially that wicked power of attraction and the irresistible handsome look. Finally, Sandy was convinced it was Jacob Grinder.

"This has to be Jacob," Sandy thought to herself. "Few people ever saw the Grinders in such open public places, anyway." As she floated in her thoughts, Jumbo brought her back to life by inviting her to come home with him to get close to the Grinders. It was an offer no woman in the state of Calazar would refuse. She quickly agreed, rejoicing in her heart. Then Jumbo nodded to his guard and he began to make space through the crowd while radioing for backup security to help get them out of there safely. As they reached the car, Jumbo for the first time realized the greatness of Sandy's beauty. He considered not only her looks but also her curves, her 5 feet 10 inches height with long, braided and free-flowing black hair. He noticed her 175 to 180 pounds weight which stressed her large and well-rounded buttocks. She also had an unblemished ebony complexion, and a figure '8' waist to match her majestic gait. As he continued to assess her, he noticed she wore at least a size 34F bra but no more than 36F. And her hips were wide, maybe 42 inches, and just the perfect size that heated up his emotions for a woman.

"She even walks like a queen," he muttered silently to himself. "What a beautiful queen. I will show this one to Mother. She would be so proud of me." Jumbo Grinder had fallen in love with this strange woman and he knew it.

When they got to Palisades Avenue they turned into the mansion at the end of the avenue, 200 Palisades Avenue, and drove straight to the back of the main house using the side driveway. As they got out of the car, the maid came out of the back of the main house to inform Jumbo that her boss, Jacklyn, had traveled and was not expected back for three days. As the driver and guard finished parking the car and refreshing themselves they came into the detached suite at the back of the main house. They sought and received his permission to leave for the night. It was just Jumbo, his guest, the maid in the main house and the two guards at the gate of the mansion left in the house. The two lovebirds wasted no time in getting down to business. They first danced to a few romantic and sexually-charged songs. The song that was playing that night was Marvin Gaye's 'Sexual Healing,' to which they danced to for sixty minutes before the sex hormones reached climax. As they got in bed and began their sexual escapades, it seemed to be business as usual for Jumbo. He had never spent a weekend without a woman in his bed or at least in his suite. Jumbo Grinder had a reputation for being smooth and cool in bed with women. After ten minutes with Jumbo on top of sandy, she quietly pulled her head towards his right ear as if to tell him something important that could not wait. At that point, Jumbo's cellphone started ringing and he cursed for not turning off the 'damned thing' before starting. He decided to ignore it and continue. The phone kept on ringing throughout this time. As her lips touched his right ear, she spoke in a soft tone despite all the moaning occurring.

"You know, Jacob Grinder, only Satan truly deserves to have the soul of Cretania. Your god, you, your fellow chosen fools with your bow and arrows, as many as you may have, can never save this land. Goodbye, Jacob Grinder." As she finished speaking, she noticed he may have not even heard her, but that was okay. But Jumbo heard just enough to pick out the words 'fools' and 'goodbye' from her speech and that troubled him a little. At first he thought she was just playing and getting into the passion because she was dying with the ecstasy and pleasure of the sex. But his military training and background had taught him to be alert and not take any word for granted. And even more especially in such a situation where he hardly knew the identity of his guest. Jumbo got up off her to take a look at her face and countenance to investigate why the sudden change of speech. At once, he noticed a sharp pain in his chest and he collapsed on top of Sandy. It felt as though a sharp knife had been plunged into his heart. As he slipped out of his body, he began to see things in the spirit and he discovered his hunch was correct. He saw a 25-inch sword go right through his heart and exit through his back. Jumbo tried to scream for help but the words were muffled and he suspected no one would hear him anyway. At the same time he turned to look at Sandy with shock written all over his face. But by this time it was not his gorgeous Sandy lying there anymore. Sandy had changed to a beautiful beast with the top half of her body still Sandy's but the bottom half the body of a serpent.

He tried to launch out to get her hair and strangle the beast, but he was too powerless even though she made no attempts to move.

Jumbo's spirit ran to the main house to fetch his mother or anyone there to inform them and get them to come and save him but there was no one there. All the guards who normally never left their posts were all gone. His spirit dashed to the family coven to alert his mother or anyone there but his mother was not there. But those who were there at once raised an alarm and rushed to 200 Palisades Avenue to try to save him. His soul, however, had begun its descent to hell, and it had crossed the threshold of return. And that meant that there was no returning of his soul back to his body. In his spirit he began to see his whole life flash before him and the memories of his mother and all his friends and girlfriends began to appear before him. His mother's soul was now on alert and she had reached his suite screaming aloud at the top of her voice in a confused and uncontrollable hysteria. As he slumped back on the bed lifeless, the strange beast gently moved from the bed and once again became Sandy. She immediately left the suite amid the screams of the many souls gathering in the suite. Sandy hurried through the driveway to the back of the house and disappeared through the back gates. Jacklyn and the group of souls which were now gathering at the suite began their pursuit.

****

The summer fellowships and prayer meetings at the Mount Zion Pentecostal in Shiloh were held on the first and middle days of the month. These days fell on the first and fifteenth day of every month throughout the summer months. On this day which was the 1st day of July there was a prayer fellowship scheduled to hold as usual between the hours of 6 p.m. and 8 p.m. in the evenings. Both Nino and Mimi had been called to testify about the events of the night two weeks ago when Nino was severely attacked as he slept at about midnight. It was their first meeting since two weeks ago when they had to do a night vigil at Nino's home after the fellowship of that day. Mount Zion Pentecostal was located on Church Street in downtown Shiloh where at least five other non-Pentecostal churches located their headquarters or regional branches. These churches were huge and were mainly of the protestant denominations namely Baptist, Methodist and Anglican. The Catholic Church was the only non-protestant church among them. It was probably just sheer coincidence that on July 1st, most of these churches were having one annual convention or the other. It was a belief in Cretania that was strongly held in Shiloh State. On the first day of the second half of the year all the requests for the rest of the year made to Jesus would be granted. All Christians were out in full force on that day to be in their churches to make prayer requests to their god. It was also no coincidence that all the churches ended their programs at about the same time which was 8 p.m. to 8:30 p.m. in the evenings. This was always the case whether the day fell on a weekday or on a weekend. Because of these events, many of the attendees shared the same parking lots even though those lots belonged to other churches besides their own.

As they left their church building, Nino and Mimi walked side by side still beaming with joy at their recent engagement two weeks ago. They were happy to finally tie the knot which was set for the upper weekend only just a few days away now. As they stepped into the open parking lot by the side of the building close to the street curb, Mimi whispered something to Nino. "There's a funny feeling I am getting and it's been like this since this morning." Nino immediately lifted his walking stick which he had been carrying since the attack a few weeks ago. Nino hit the stick against the nearest wall as though signaling his readiness for any unforeseen situation.

He hadn't mentioned a word to Mimi about the incidents with the mirror and Melina. He planned to find out certain information about his mother's family first. As they entered the building of the Mount Zion parking lot they walked towards the elevator to get to the highest floor which was the seventh floor. As they reached their destination floor, they got out and began walking to their car. There were many other church attendees who were also trying to get to their cars and leave for the night. There were many more people who had reached their cars and were driving them through the driveway towards the direction of the floor exit. Nino and Mimi reached the second row of cars on their way to get to the tenth row where their car was parked. Suddenly there was a shrill and deafening cry which at first seemed to come from above but actually came from nowhere in particular. Nino and Mimi had to stopper their ears due to the sharp piercing effect of the sound. Many other car owners had to do the same to avoid hearing the sharp sound which sounded like an evil summon from the spirits of the grave and death. As Mimi covered her ears she lifted her head to look in the direction of the skies. She immediately noticed what seemed to be a medium-sized black bird flying in a circle over the area of the parking lot just above them. She hit Nino, who was by this time on one knee on the floor, with her shoulder without removing her hands from her ears and he turned to look at her. She then gestured to him to look at the bird flying in the sky which was the source of the wicked sound that was tormenting them. The sound stabbed at their souls and spirits as if it was trying to rip them out of their bodies by force. As Nino tried to focus his eyes into the darkness of the skies above to calculate the distance between him and the bird, he noticed the sound was no ordinary sound. His strength was ebbing and an overwhelming fatigue had overcome him. It was like the attack that occurred a few weeks ago all over again. He tried to get up and take aim at the evil bird and throw the stick like a javelin to kill the bird. But the bird was moving too fast overhead. And besides, the sound was draining more energy with every second it persisted. In the corner of their eyes both Nino and Mimi could see a few of the other car owners were on the floor, some of them writhing in pain and others lying motionless. As Nino knelt on that floor he noticed he could summon some strength as he prayed within his mind. Then he slowly got up and once again took aim at the bird which was now flying much slower and lower as though it was tiring out or had attained its goal.

As Nino drew closer to the nearby wall to steady himself and prepare a projectile using the rod, he lost his grip on the rod and it dropped to what he hoped would be the sixth floor. As he looked down to see where the stick had fallen he noticed a mysterious person, a strange figure standing beside the rod who picked it up from the floor. He couldn't make out the face, shape or gender of this mysterious person but he hoped he or she was a friend. But then he noticed something that startled him and almost frightened him. The figure had no shadow in the floor light and was not covering any of its ears as if the bird sounds had no effect on its soul or spirit. As the figure came close to the rod, it didn't look up at anyone as though Nino and the others weren't even there. And as Nino pondered these things, the figure picked up the rod and looked up at the black bird. The bird now flew round and round and was just about 50 meters above the seventh floor and a few more meters above the sixth floor. With great force the figure threw the rod upwards like a javelin in the general direction of the bird. As the rod left the hand of the stranger it turned into a two-edged sword about five feet long. It flew like it was a laser-guided missile surrounded by flames of fire rushing with perfect precision toward its target. About seven seconds later it was all over as the sword smashed into the bird with its blade cutting of the head of the bird. The effect was instantaneous as the death cry immediately stopped. The bird fell down in a straight path on the car belonging to Nino.

Mimi sat on the floor with her legs folded up and her face hidden in her legs. She kept her hands on her ears and there was a halo around her as she sat on the floor. Nino went over to her and picked her up while informing her that the ordeal had ended. It was a terrible scene at the parking lot and Nino and Mimi gathered themselves together and stood transfixed to the spot. As they looked around they noticed at least twenty-four bodies lying lifeless on the parking floor. The first responders, paramedics and the police had arrived and were slowly going from person to person assessing the people and situation. It took about an hour for the couple to finish giving initial eyewitness accounts. Nino looked around and noticed the strange figure was gone and the rod was just a couple of meters from his feet. As he wondered what it all meant, Mimi who had also observed what happened understood all that had occurred.

As they got to their car, there was the headless black bird still on the sun roof of their 2005 Hummer H2 and it was hard as stone. On close inspection they found that it was a raven, but it was much larger than the normal size for the bird. Nino quickly used the rod to push the bird off the car and pushed it to the ground where he burnt it to ashes.

A few days later there was a call on Nino's cellphone and it was his father Benjamin. His father just called to inform him that there had been a few deaths in the family in the past few days. Five members of the family had just died — two on Benjamin's side and three on Maraya's side. It was Maraya's notoriously wicked age-defying aunt and the remaining two of her brothers, who were uncles of Maraya's, who had died. And on his side of the family the deceased were Benjamin's youngest brother, John Joe, and his wife. Nino tried to grieve but a great feeling of joy and satisfaction came over him as he informed his fiancée. And his father ended the call by telling him, "Now our life begins, son."

CHAPTER TEN

A Gathering of Thorns

The rebellion against righteousness in the great nation of Cretania ran quite deep. It was probably as deep as the root system of the Oak, or some other deep-rooted, tree. The most intriguing thing was the relatively short time that this deep root system had formed. The most troubling thing was that throughout these developments, as bad as they were, the good people of Cretania were mostly ignorant about them. There was an attitude of complacency and ignorant comfort concerning these evil plots to uproot godliness from the Cretan society. It was unfortunate, but true, that the evil plans had succeeded to a large extent and were still succeeding. As the resistance from light became stronger, darkness didn't relent but increased its power and efforts. As a result, there was now a war which had entered its final stages and had begun to approach its climax. The evil powers working in Cretania had become like an evil tree with so many roots and branches which produced the bitterest fruits. And it threatened to take over the whole vineyard of Cretania.

The wicked tree of Cretania was determined to spread its branches throughout the country and take over every part. They had one quality which gave them a false sense of future victory. And that quality was that their organization was built upon a well-defined military hierarchy. There were three levels of power in the sub-kingdom of darkness overruling the Cretanian nation. The highest level was the most powerful and it was a group that comprised the five most powerful men in the country coordinating activities and projects that controlled the nation. This group of men was overseen by the most powerful being in the country. He was the King of the dark Cretan kingdom who sat above the hierarchy of power and command.

It was none other than the Legionnaire who went by his real name of Zebulon. He was overseer of the most dangerous, most influential and very powerful Pentosi. Because of the exclusivity of the Pentosi, most of the powerful men of Cretania couldn't be members of the group. The lesser souls who would be a part of this evil hierarchy had to settle for something lesser and inferior to the highest group. The second group was the unisex group of power brokers that was started by the king, Zebulon, when he realized the need for such a society. He intuitively called it The Society and destined it to become the go-between linking the first and third groups in the power hierarchy. The Society was subdivided based on certain factors into discrete units called clans. It comprised most of the powerful and influential men and women in the Cretanian society. This included politicians, business tycoons, scientists, artists, colonels, generals, investors, financiers and economists. They had physical branches where they met on a strict schedule. When they began, the members only met in the spiritual realm and only on a strict schedule created by the leaders of a clan or the two highest spirits, Zebulon and Malachiel.

The last and lowest of the hierarchy was the witchcraft society. This comprised all the other members who were not ranking in any way. The members of this level were the rank-and-file, the so-called floor members. The people who mattered in Cretania were in either of the first two levels of the kingdom's power hierarchy. Everybody else that was part of the dark kingdom in Cretania was a member of this last group. This was the base, the foundation, the common denominator for anyone who was a part of this kingdom. One unique thing about this level was that they always played host to everyone whenever there was a general convention in the dark kingdom of Cretania. The convention occurred once every three years, and that time had come again. It was now the penultimate year of the second, and last, term of President Samuel Everlast.

The Crestar River was one of the few distributaries given off from the Yellow River. As the great river ran its course through the northern Cretanian region just about the middle border of Crestar City, it gave off this small river. The river at once veered right towards the center of the border of Crestar City. River Crestar ran for about 100 kilometers into the nation's capital. It ended in a rainforest swamp which was actually a collection of rainwater forests. The locals gave it the name 'forest of sounds' because of the strange sounds that were heard coming from the forests at certain times of the year. There were singing sounds, sounds of wild beasts, sounds of partying and celebration. And there were screams of terror and death. In the middle of the forest was a giant Ceiba tree that was at least 35 meters in radius. It grew hundreds of feet into the air and had hundreds of branches. This tree had the rare distinction of being a national meeting place of the lowest level of Cretania's dark peoples.

This day was the last working day of the second quarter of the year. It was a year that had seen so much chaos in political circles especially in the presidency and in the life of the president himself. It was a Friday and it was chosen to be the day for the convention. On the appointed day, it was business as usual as citizens went about their normal daily routines.

The attendees began arriving at exactly 12 a.m. by midnight West Central Yellow River Time. The highest members arrived on time and they positioned themselves separately from the rest of the crowd. On the top of the hill stood the king, prince and other spirit dignitaries together with their legions. The special guest of honor invited was the outgoing president's Chief of Army Staff. He was Lieutenant General Ferdinand Gyros. He was also requested to bring his wife to the hilltop executive seating. She was none other than the only daughter of the Quartosian president, General Cain Cosmos. Her name was Georgina Marilyn 'Gigi'

Cosmos Gyros, and she had recently become a top celebrity in the kingdom. Many believed she should become the spokesperson for women's rights because of her beauty, influence and charisma. So many Cretanians thought it strange that the previously unknown wife of the head of the country's army would suddenly become so popular. Her popularity ratings were now even higher than that of the First Lady, Priscilla Strongbow. There were even rumors going around that Mrs. Gyros was the queen that would preside over Cretania in the future. But many warned that the prophecy spoke of a 'Queen of Thorns' who would do so much damage to the country that she would rip apart the flesh of the nation. It was these sorts of rumors, support and beliefs about her that made Georgina Gyros the enigma she was, and the legend that was slowly but surely rising.

It was a must for all members of The Society to be present at this grand convention but only the highest members were permitted on the hilltop. All other members were expected to be in the crowd. And it was a large crowd indeed. All the top members of the various clans of the society and the leaders of the lowest hierarchy groups around the country were present. The members of the Pentosi chose whether or not to appear at this or any meeting—and they often chose not to appear. If they did appear, it was always in strict anonymity. The king and the crown prince stood in the center of the hilltop that was reserved for high royalty. Both of them had their legions surrounding them all around like bees around their queen. Zebulon stood in the middle of the central hilltop while Malachiel was at the bottom of the hilltop royal circle. The king was the only part of the Pentosi permitted to be here as the identity of the chairs was a forbidden taboo in all Cretania. The purpose of this meeting was to inform the citizens of the kingdom that there was a great movement imminent in the country. But most important was the introduction of the new human leaders of the kingdom. Unknown to many attendees, this was the "night of the changeover."

At exactly 1 a.m., the Legionnaire called for the beginning of the meeting and there was calm. All attendees now focused on the king and the crown prince as they addressed the convention. It was the king who began speaking and did all the talking.

"My people of this great nation of Cretania, I salute you. It has been nearly three years since we last gathered here. The last time I informed you all about the great progress we are making to take over this nation. I then told you about the big changes to be made for these plans to be a success. The new changes are needed for us to plant ourselves firmly in this land and to remove all opposition to our rule. The changes are for the purposes of extinguishing the light. Once we do that, all the wealth, all the power, all the milk and honey in this land will surely become our own. Then there shall be no need for any BSQ, godliness or even righteousness. We can do what we want, how we want and wherever we want. All our people who need blood for one goal or the other can have all the blood they need. It is unfortunate that we should have been here over three years ago but the great one who should have led our forces to that victory has failed us. And we must let him suffer the full brunt of the consequences of failing this kingdom. I will not mention any names but it's one of the main reasons we are here tonight. We are here because we have chosen the new men and women who will be your leaders to achieve victory in our next series of battles. Once we meet our goal in the next major battle, we shall gather again and then you will be informed what to do then. Until then know that these are the days of fierce war and it's a war we have won already. We will redefine the meaning of death in these strange lands. Soon the people of this country will hear and run to obey our every wish and command. Soon we shall have no other people in Cretania but our own people and we shall control everything." At these last words there was uproar from all the attendees both on the hill and down below. The Legion King paused for about 45 seconds and then he continued his speech.

"This nation of Cretania is well worth the war. I shall make no deceptions, my dear ones, there will be casualties. There will be deaths on our side and there will be deaths on their side. But that is irrelevant to the great cause we pursue. Because once this land belongs to us we shall have the richest nation per capita in the whole world. And we shall have one of the most beautiful countries on earth today and the most magnificent one in the future. Those who come into this country shall become slaves to us and servants to our ways. We shall rule the world from Crestar City, Cretania."

Again, there was more applause but this time a thunderous one. And the Legion King responded to the applause by looking up to heavens and roaring out great balls of fire. His head had transformed into the head of a lion and his mane stood up erect. After about fifteen to twenty minutes of this showmanship, Zebulon continued with his lengthy speech.

"I won't take any more of your time. Now I will introduce the men and women that will soon be in control of the people of Cretania." The Legionnaire began to introduce men and women who were gathered around the hilltop. There was no reason given for any of the introductions. It was generally expected that all members were wise enough to discern what was happening from their local groups. Some of them were familiar to the crowd but most of them were not. Finally, it came down to the introduction of the last man and woman on the list of members to be introduced.

"Finally, I shall introduce the man most of you should know quite well. He is the right-hand man of your great president, Samuel Everlast. This man is the greatest soldier in the land and the main henchman for the president. He is General

Ferdinand Gyros." All the members of the Cretanian Armed Forces in the crowd gave the army boss a standing ovation. So also did everyone who knew him or were familiar with his great career achievements. General Gyros turned to face the crowd and made a small speech that wowed and fired up the crowd.

"Great people of Cretania, the time's now come when one kingdom must unite to dispossess another one of a high-value property. We do not have to be the original owners or creators. The kingdom of Zebulon comprises true soldiers and not true cowards, takers not creators, victors and not victims, and killers not corpses. We are strong winds filled with power of death. We blow on the enemy and they turn to dust. Ashes to ashes and dust to dust, from dust they came and back to dust they shall go."

As General Gyros finished his speech, the crowd was screaming at the top of their voices. It was as though they had just been set on fire. The tyranny of death that stood before them couldn't discourage them in the slightest. Or maybe it was because they did not understand what exactly was before them. Some in that same crowd who knew the general's military career history were terrified at what just transpired. They knew his introduction at the last meant only one thing for Cretania and they wisely kept silent. But the king continued to the final introduction and this was something that surprised everyone. The last introduction was always reserved for the general who was chosen to lead the war. But again, none of the suspicious souls dared say a word or show any sign of suspicion or understanding. To do so would mean only one thing and that was a certain death for them and their families. Zebulon continued with his hosting duties after the applause had died down.

"The last but not the least is a woman many of you know too well. She is the most beloved woman in this kingdom and is more popular nationwide than the First Lady, Strongbow. She is the chief adviser of the previous speaker and is actually his own sweetheart and wife. I now give you your queen, the great, beautiful and irresistible Gigi Gyros."

There were only a few in the whole crowd or on the hill who did not know or hadn't heard about Georgina Gyros. She was the daughter of the infamous Quartosian strongman, General Cain

Cosmos. He was the rebellious general who seized power in the nation of Quartos and had governed it for over 35 years. Those who knew their family saw her as her father's right hand and sometimes executioner.

A popular story had it that once there was a rebellion against her father's regime, and some of the top officers under her father were involved in a putsch against him. At the height of the rebellion, Gigi went to her father and told him to proceed on his annual holiday as usual and leave the battle to her. She promised her father that in thirty days, she would present him with the heads of all the leaders of the rebellion. "I need only thirty days for all I need to do with these ungrateful dogs, father. Just give me thirty days and no more."

At first some of her father's top generals counseled against it but President Cosmos knew the kind of daughter he had. He went ahead to leave the country for his holiday to the distant European nation of France. Gigi retired all the top generals and brought together the two most reliable colonels under her father. Colonel Abel Luomo and Colonel George Sanders came to see the female military strategist. And after three days of deliberation, they formulated a great strategy. They separated the rebels into three groups and they each chose one of the groups to execute their strategy. The first group was led by General Fred Heath, the former Chief of the Army. The second group was led by General Frank Benton, the deputy Chief of the Armed Forces. The third rebel group was led by the one-time friend of President Cosmos—General Papa Lux. General Lux was the commander of all the rebels because he had the greatest seniority, experience and closeness to the president. According to plan, Gigi took on Lux. Luomo took on his former boss General Benton while Sanders was assigned General Heath. Each one of them was given a different strategy with which to destroy their targets. The plan was simple, and it was to use their targets' greatest weakness to destroy them and kill their men. Heath was in it mainly for the money. So Sanders was given the equivalent of 15 million cretari to offer his target to give up the rebellion and flee to an unknown destination. Benton was in it for the political power. So Gigi coached Luomo to convince him to accept the position of vice president with a convincing proposal that would deceive him. As for Lux he too was in it for the money but also for power. But General Lux had a greater weakness—sex with beautiful and powerful women. So they dangled all his weaknesses before him though the real plan was to give him just one—a beautiful and powerful woman. The woman being offered was Gigi herself. She convinced Lux she was no longer on friendly terms with her father, and she too had defected from him.

With these strategies, the three of them went to work. They knew the first part of the battle was to make them part ways for whatever reason they could find. The then Lady Cosmos and her colonels understood that separating true generals in times of war was a daunting and almost impossible task. Each one of three strategists used decoys to mask their true identities. Only when proof was needed of the validity of the proposals were they to come into the picture.

"These generals are not true generals but godforsaken opportunists and ingrates," Gigi had bursted out in anger during one of the strategy sessions with her men. "My father has made all his generals comfortable and fed fat and they dare do this. I shall butcher that Lux like he is a pig, that fat ungrateful murderer," President Cosmos' daughter screamed out sounding very irritated and impatient. "We shall kill them, Madame Cosmos, because there is no escaping us now. We need just a little patience now," said Colonel Luomo speaking in his typical French accent.

As they finished that session, they got news that Generals Heath and Benton had been separated and were willing to meet with their different contacts. Even they would not have guessed they were walking into their death traps. It took two weeks to separate the generals and their men but it took only eleven days more to destroy the generals. The last of the generals to be killed was Lux, and he died two hours after a 24-hour marathon sex session with Gigi herself. The general had bought her story in the heat of the temptation. Having sex with Georgina Cosmos had always been one of his biggest desires. He couldn't throw away this chance to have and own all the things he ever wanted. But he should have known better. None of his colleagues could discern the evil plot against them either. With the president out of the country, it all seemed so real.

Such was the power, brilliance and influence of the great Georgina Cosmos. Her father, President Cosmos, came back from his trip about five days short of the anticipated thirty days. She presented him with the heads of the rebel leaders with each one on a spike and a circular plaiting of thorns on their heads. She became the most powerful woman in the country ever since those days. Her father made her the Quartosian Chief Security Adviser for her wisdom and fearlessness in state, security and military matters. After that incident she became greatly feared not only in Quartos but also in Yellow River. Not only was she a brilliant strategist, she was also quite religious and most spiritual. Gigi believed that to be a controller of peoples, you had to be on top of matters that historically were known to have the power to congregate peoples. Anyone who controlled these subjects would control their congregations. It was this ideology that was inculcated in her by her mother that drove her to master the main books of the world's main religions. By the time she turned 18, she had studied and mastered the Bible, the Koran and the Bhagavad Gita. She had never lost any competition of recital of verses of religious books.

When Gigi was 15 years old, there was a great prophecy by one of the seers in her native Quartos. The prophecy said that she was "destined to be a queen in her own kingdom and not under her father, but that kingdom will be in a foreign land where she shall be in control of a foreign people." There was something else she had never entered and lost in all her life and that was poetry competitions. She was a gifted poet, and many who knew her felt it was this more than her beauty that accentuated her charisma. Her poems were as prophetic as they were beautiful and many saw her as a great prophetess. By the time she was 30 years old she had been nominated as one of the national poet laureates of her native country. It was a nomination which she jointly won with the great poet, Sherman the Elder. Sherman was reputed to be one of the greatest Quartosian poets of all time. But many Quartosian people attributed Gigi's success as a poet to her father's position and power. By the time she turned 30 years, thirty-two of the greatest men and children of the greatest men around the world had proposed marriage to her. Countless more had tried to take her to bed, but failed in their bid. Naturally, she was hard to get but once she loved or needed a man, Gigi was a wide open book. As far as Gigi was concerned, destiny came first in her life. Every other thing, including love, came after that primary priority. That was the way her father had taught her. Whether it was in fulfillment of prophecy or it was the call of destiny, she met and fell in love with the son of a Greek merchant based in Cretania. The merchant was then on a business trip around Yellow River with his children. The merchant brought his children along for a presidential lunch for business people, business owners, dignitaries and foreign government officials in Quartos. This Cretanian merchant was named Alanio Gyros and his son was Captain Ferdinand Gyros of the Cretanian Army. As soon as Captain Gyros met Gigi Cosmos, he tried to date her. He failed at first but finally succeeded.

****

The incident of the failed military coup d'état in the North Yellow River nation of Quartos occurred over 15 years ago. She was now Mrs.

Georgina Marilyn Gyros, the wife of the leader of the army soldiers in Cretania. When they got married, they adopted a seal of a golden crown with diamonds shaped like thorns sitting at the top pointed ends of the crown. She knew she had to give a speech tonight, and she was ready with a poem. On this night as she approached the top of the hilltop she had a little time to reminisce and think of her life's journey so far. It was all going according to plan she assured herself mentally as she took a quick glance around the hilltop. She noticed that all her people were there as planned. She noticed her father, President Cosmos, her mother, Tamara, her junior brothers, Sunny and Maximus, uncles, aunts and in-laws. And, of course, there was her husband, General Gyros. As she ran her eyes to and fro she noticed that the First Lady, Mrs. Priscilla Strongbow-Everlast, was conspicuously absent. That was strange and funny, she thought to herself. But she was too focused to be distracted by such issues. As she got on the stage she bursted out laughing in her usual infectious laughter which she used to woo the crowds and captivate them. She began with a series of "thank you" salutations blown into the crowd as kisses.

And then she started laying out her rhymes as the gentle winds continued blowing. She gave her poetic speech in two verses:

"May the gentle winds wrap calm around your naked soul,
As the eternal forces lock horns and battle for control,
The cut of the double-edged sword versus the stinging of bees as they sing,
The arrow of the skilled bowman versus the stubborn scorpions' sting,
The quenching power of the dark waters versus the spontaneous fire that only grows hotter,
The sweetness and freedom of sin versus the insipid and strict ways of the righteous one,
The dark powers of the moon light versus the burning fires of the midday sun,
Ignorance and comfort in the midst of the thorn,
Beauty and gentleness under siege of the dark-born,
Through this way a war of attrition comes along,
Pray we partake of the outcome with the victor's song,
So take your sides and brace for eternity's goal,

And may the gentle winds wrap peace around your dark soul."

"May the breeze of anticipation wrap calm around your hopeful soul,
May your enemies' fall crown your victory in quest for your wicked goal,
But it's the joy of reclaimed possessions versus the sweetness of spoils of war,
It's the conquest of the great queen or the power of the chosen sword,
It's the devastation of the eye of the storm versus the still calm of the peaceful seas,
It's consumption by the holy fires or death by the sting of the killer bees,
The pretty ones falling under unholy deceit,
Clear signs that none beloved could interpret,
Ignorance turns a sword that slays the unseeing heart,
The quicker the weapons the sooner the enemy is torn apart,
Under the cover of love unleash the thorns,
While the pretty ones sleep and turn,
The Cretan forces mighty and crafty,

The forces of third heavens troubled already,
Through this way a war of retribution comes along,
Pray we conquer all to join in the victor's song,
So take your sides and ready for destiny's role,
And may this gentle breeze wrap victory around
your dark, dark soul."

It took Mrs. Gyros about twelve minutes to end her poetic speech. As she finished, the spirits were the first to applaud her great effort and soon everyone else joined in for a standing ovation. As soon as the clock struck 3 a.m., the meeting place was totally empty and no more sounds were heard in the forest that night.

EPILOGUE

The Rains of Mystery River

"Release the stones, release the stones now," was the shout of the thunderous voice of the demon king. He stood on his throne staring down towards the earth from an aerial view of the whole country that was his kingdom.

"The stones do fly, my Lord. ETA to Mystery River is 60 minutes by earth's time," was the reply from the chief warrior who stood on the steps of the throne just two flights below the king. The warriors released them all at once with great might and their visages showed they were filled with great wrath making their thrust all the more powerful. As the stones slowly left, the fires burning in them left embers which scorched anything in their path as they traveled downward. Their primary destination was the city of Mystery River in the nation of Cretania. As they all watched the stones as they hurtled down to earth, the princes all arose with one accord and praised their king, Zebulon. Afterward, they also praised the Prince of Darkness who is also known as the Prince of the World and Satan. They sang the song of warriors going to war.

"Who, who, who shall stand against us,
Against the king, and against the princes,
Winds of death go whirl and whirl,
Woe to man, woman, boy and girl,
Their flesh and blood devour we well,
And their souls will descend to fiery hell."

As they sang this and other songs, they entered their ships and airplanes and they headed towards the earth to their destination. The princes entered the same vehicles as their legions of warriors and they took the executive positions. The king stood with his own legions and bid them farewell with his usual song as they left. It was customary for the king to watch the events unfold on earth from his throne in the second heavens as it all unfolded on earth.

Many of the princes, and even the king who was also called Legionnaire, had many physical features of mankind. But in their natural form they were all giants and had many anatomical features that differentiated them from humanity. Some of them had more than one pair of eyes, others had tails and others were hybrids of man and animals. As for the warriors, they were mostly morbid beasts that were better not seen with the naked human eyes. They were horrifying to look at by any human or earthly standards. Most of them were hybrid combinations of two or more animals, including humans. Others were in the form of animals and yet others were in the form of trees and plants. They all had various colors and those colors were in different tones and hues. Some had many eyes and ears and those with multiple senses had those senses facing different directions. Some eyes faced upwards and others backwards and others faced sideways. Many of them had multiple appendages–multiple hands, legs and heads. The warriors were giants and the shortest in height was 100 feet tall. Each of the princes had a legion of warriors assigned to him and they usually were about 20 legions for each prince. The chief prince was Malachiel, and he had the highest number of legions, about 50, of all the princes but less than the king. All warriors were ultimately under the authority of the Zebulon who had 70 dedicated legions under his authority. Both princes and warriors had a pair of gigantic ancient swords strapped to their sides. They also had other weapons with which they armed themselves to the teeth just in case of any resistance.

"Cretania is known for its many angels going to and fro," the Legion King barked at his legions. "So arm yourselves to the death for there will be no going back. Possess your own powerful and deadly stones. It's now or never—either we take Cretania now or maybe never again." The thoughts of the king paced back and forth as he tried to stay on top of the plans and make sure there were no loose ends.

The stones comprised large rocks plucked from the grounds of the kingdom, from the meteors, rocks that float around with the stars and the stars themselves. They were gathered in one place and had all been set on fire by the blast of breath from the princes and the king himself. They had been gathering these rocks for many years in preparation for this day which was the build-up to the climax of the war for the soul of Cretania. Cretania was not only the most powerful nation in the continental Yellow River but it was also the most resistant to the works of darkness. And not only that, it was the most populous, after the nation of Quartos, and by far the most powerful economically and politically. And whoever controlled Cretania would wield great influence economically and otherwise over the whole continent. It was a prize that was worth fighting for by any standards. The smallest rocks were averaging anywhere in size from two to five tons, the medium stones from 30 tons to 70 tons and largest ones north of 100 tons. And some rocks were as large as earthly mountains by standard human measurements. With the size and the velocity at which they were traveling they were sure to have an impact that would rattle the foundations of the whole Cretania.

This battle had been raging for many years and the big breakthrough came fifty years ago when the people of the dark side got a member of the most powerful organization of the country, the Pentosi, in the highest office in the land. But things did not go as planned for the past five to seven years because the current president turned against the powers of the kingdom, biting the hands that fed him and made him great. So there was a slight change of plans, and the new plan was to destroy the presidency including the president, and take over the country. They would then bring in a new leader who will be loyal to the kingdom. In the process they would put the country in a state where it will never be within the grasp of the righteous people ever again. Much blood had to be shed and it had to be done in a way that it would look as though it was a punishment by the highest of all gods. So that the people of the country will see the aftermath as being by the divine will of the same god. King Zebulon ran the plan in his mind over and over again.

The king had personally chosen the next president and he was certain there will be no disappointment this time. And it was even more comforting to know that his wife was the most powerful daughter of the family in Yellow River. The warriors were highly trained in their areas of expertise. These expertise included killing and wasting humanity, battling the angels of the kingdom of heaven and giving the people of the dark kingdom power and skill to destroy their counterparts in the kingdom of light.

The city of Mystery River was in the northern part of the state of Happyness and it had been chosen because it was seen as a talisman for the nation. There was a belief that those who settled down successfully in Happyness were blessed by Jesus and they have great destinies from heaven. If an evil person tried to settle down in Happyness they would meet with unpleasant circumstances and perhaps even tragedy. It was an omen so many tried to take advantage of so they could exploit the great financial and other opportunities in the state. The greatest mystery in the state was that a river whose waters had great powers mysteriously came from an unknown source and ended up in the great Yellow River. This river which was called Mystery River became the name of the city where it began. The legend of Mystery River began during the great epidemic called Sepsis when there was no fresh potable water in the country and people were dying of water poisoning and thirst. The leaders of the country at that time then declared a day of prayer and fasting and by the next morning a large flowing river had appeared in the city where the prayers were made. The river had no source but its water was fresh and drinkable. It supplied the whole nation until the end of the epidemic when normal water filtration resumed. That city was Mystery River and from that day many citizens preferred to call it 'Miracle River.' Its water was believed to be the blood that supplied the nation and kept it alive. The river was known to cure diseases and heal anyone or anything that drank of its waters.

For these reasons, the convention organizers chose to hold their meeting in Mystery River. But it was not only for that reason the organizers chose the city for their meeting. It was also believed that whatever started in Mystery River would be conferred with immortality. And it was partly because of what this belief would symbolize for their cause that they chose Mystery River. That way, their cause probably will live forever in Cretania and become widely accepted by all its citizens. It was not only a dangerous gamble to take, but it was something those who knew and understood the mysteries of the city warned against but to no avail. The organizers were warned that it would be a terrible insult to God and it would bring dire consequences but their warnings went unheeded. It was perceived that Mystery River was the primary ancient gate that led straight to the throne of Jehovah in the highest heavens.

On this fateful day the stars and elements in the second heavens all seemed to be in support of the powers of darkness over Cretania. It was the hour of darkness over the nation of Cretania, and the stars arrayed themselves beautifully while murmuring to one another about the consequences of this matter. Some were obviously fearful of the certain retaliation from the highest heavens. Others were simply unconcerned and put up an attitude of nonchalance. Most stars looked beautiful but frightened but all the elements sang, in one accord, the song of damnation–the damnation of the great nation of Cretania. But there was something they all agreed upon-this day was long overdue and the people of Cretania had been asking for this for a long time now. The stars cursed the sinners of Cretania for nothing other than the darkness they brought upon the once beautiful soul of the nation because of their sins. As the warriors chanted the song of war, they prepared to descend to earth and finish the work started by the rocks.

As the fiery stones rushed towards their target on the earth, the armada of warriors and princes followed closely behind. They traveled at the lightning speed covering thousands of miles every minute. Whatever the stones did not destroy the warriors would destroy. Whatever the warriors missed the leaders of darkness in the country would destroy. So the most powerful human citizens of the dark kingdom will tie up all loose ends. Their goal was simple—destroy every remaining ray of light and blame it on the God of light. And then sit back and let the Christians and other people of the light suffer the backlash.

It was the night of the Great Moon, the first full moon which coincided with the largest appearance of the moon for the year. The people of the nation called such an occurrence a super moon. That day fell on a Friday and the previous day fell on the thirteenth day of the month. Far away in Mystery River City, there was pomp and pageantry in the main event going on in the city. It was the second day of the convention and there was great joy in the hearts of the attendees. They knew this convention marked a major breakthrough in the struggle of queer peoples in the world to achieve legitimacy and acceptance by the people of the world. All the leaders of the various groups and mayors of the cities who were part of this struggle were all present. They came not only from Yellow River but different parts of the world. The First Lady was rumored to be in the city but had not shown herself in the convention center. But another rumor had it that she was there in the city but chose to be anonymous so as not to jeopardize her husband's presidency. And it was also to save herself the almost certain death threats and attempts on her life that she would attract if she showed up in person. Yet another rumor had it that the First Lady had died a day before the start of the convention from a mysterious illness. And another one had it that she had been assassinated by powerful forces working against her husband, the president. When the rumors about the First Lady's presence circulated, it lifted the morale of the attendees. But when the rumors of her death began to filter in, most people affiliated with the event chose not to believe. But those who believed sought the news from newspapers and radio and TV channels in attempts to verify the rumors but to no avail. There was not one single news story about the First Lady.

Despite the fact that so many attendees had come from abroad, many in the LGBTQ community in the country were still in the closet and did not dare show up for the convention. There were few people who lived such a lifestyle in the country openly. And some believed there were none at all because all members of that community were supposed to have abandoned that lifestyle or left the country altogether. The citizens of Cretania were well aware that God had issued a curse by his prophets on certain sins in the country and the gay lifestyle was one of them. They knew public display of sodomy would invite certain death on anyone who manifested that lifestyle and any private display of the lifestyle would become public in no time. Any public display of the sins of the BSQ in Cretania, even the slightest, was not tolerated and was perceived to be an invitation to death. And it was often a painful and merciless death because of

what was written in the writings of the great
prophet Eliyahu Nautilus:

"A man for a woman and a woman for each man
In the image of God, the Lord created them,
Adding them to his divine master plan,
So if any shall violate the Lord's natural form,
To seek the passion of their own kind,
Or shed the blood of an innocent man,
To take the life of one without guilt,
Or set up idols without or within,
Or take flesh and blood to buy or sell,
I, the Lord, shall destroy them for their sin,
Their souls condemned to the pits of hell."

Many of the citizens, including Christians,
tried to warn the convention organizers of this
prophecy but to no avail. None of them were
willing to listen and especially when they had the
most powerful woman in the nation on their side as
one of the organizers. None of them believed that a
decades-old prophecy by a prophet who died over
three decades ago still had any effect. Many of the

Christians and non-believers resigned themselves to the fact that this was the will of God and destiny that was inevitable in Cretania. But none of them doubted there would be grievous consequences.

About thirty minutes before the shower of the stones, the Meteorological Service of Cretania, CMS, sent an emergency facsimile to the office of the president but they got no reply from that office. The Director of the CMS was called in from holiday but couldn't come into the capital city of Crestar fast enough. As a result, the CMS Deputy Director had been called in as instructed by the director when he was informed of the nature of the emergency. No one in any of the federal ministries took the matter seriously when it first broke as something as ridiculous as this had never before happened. The CMS Deputy Director, Dr. Trina Spock, came into the office as fast as she could and she was totally shocked at the nature of the emergency. All her senior scientists on duty had assured her that there was a massive barrage of meteorites headed towards Cretania and they couldn't verify where exactly it would make landing. There were so many of them and they were arrayed in a cluster formation with a large diameter that it was hard to predict all the states that would be affected. What they knew for certain was that the states of Communitas, Eastern River, Portland and Happyness would be affected. They predicted that some of the meteors would fall into the Yellow River off the coasts of Happyness and Portland, which were the two neighboring states bordering the Yellow River closest to the Atlantic Ocean. And they also knew they would begin to make landing in about thirty minutes and no less. But they didn't know how much the various states would be affected but now it was clear that Happyness would be severely hit. Dr. Spock protested that the scientists verify the matter further as this had never happened before in Cretania and not at such short notice anywhere in the world. But the scientists assured her of what they had found. Everything happening was totally contrary to the science they learned at school and had experienced in the country before now. She asked if the president's office was aware and was assured that they had sent the message by secure fax, but there was no reply. And the same was the case for the ministries of Information and Geological and Weather Services.

And then about ten minutes later the Minister of Geological Services, Professor Herzburg, called back on the hot line and he was in obvious shock. At this time, the senior scientists had just updated Dr. Spock that the incoming objects were just about ten minutes away now. And they were now traveling at velocities that would level any city or town they landed on and make impact so deep they would shake the foundations of the states in which they landed.

"Dr. Spock, this is Professor Herzburg. Is this for real what's happening?" "Hello, Minister. Yes it is I'm afraid. We have never seen anything like this before here or anywhere in the world. It looks like a meteor shower but these meteors are so big and are moving so fast it's incredible. They should have burned out minutes ago but they are still falling and don't look like they'll burn out anytime soon. It is so strange it's unbelievable. They had to call me back to the office to handle this because the Director is away." Dr. Spock answered back hurriedly.

"The president is also away attending the global summit on international finance and development. All world leaders and their ministers are there. I sent my deputy in my stead. I will call him to inform the president over there," the minister replied. "Minister, we have only about ten minutes left and I don't know if it's enough time to alert emergency services. I have called the state governors in all states especially in those we believe will be affected and they have alerted their fire, police and first responders. You need to alert and activate the federal emergency services at once, sir."

"I have done that, Deputy Director, and they will be in touch with you shortly to get the precise details of what to expect. What people need to do now in this country is to take shelter where ever possible. I will come over to the CMS so we can have a televised conference if we have the time." "No sir we don't have the time. You are better off calling the TV and Radio stations and advising them to make their own broadcast." "As a matter of fact, the president has just called to give his permission to make those broadcasts so I will now authorize them." And those were the last words from the minister before he ended the call with Director Spock and hung up the phone.

In a few minutes the whole nation was in a frenzied state. Fear had gripped the whole nation and pandemonium had broken out. The office of the president had ordered a State of Emergency in those states predicted to be hit by the rain of falling meteorites. The broadcasts asked all citizens to "abandon whatever they were doing and take shelter in the nearest place of shelter." These shelters included under any bridge, the underground subway system, the basement of homes and buildings and in bunkers inside or outside of military bases.

At the venue of the convention, news had broken that there was a terrible thing, a natural disaster, about to happen in the city. But it was just a speculation and only some of the organizers had heard what was actually happening. Many dismissed it as a mere speculation and nothing but mere rumor to disorganize their great historical gathering. Most of them resolved to stay to the end of the proceedings of the second day which would end about 9 p.m. that evening. The penultimate speaker was just being introduced and was making his way to the stage when the time turned 6:05 p.m.

Then the great nightmare began. At exactly 6:06 p.m. the first set of rocks hit the ground in the downtown region of Mystery River. As the next set of rocks began to fall, there was death, destruction and pandemonium everywhere. It was the sound of thunder and lightning mixed with terrible shaking all happening at once. Every building in the downtown core shook with tremors so great that many people broke into pieces starting from their head and neck, thoracic and abdominal regions. Large rocks came down on the city and some of them which were in flames exploded and turned to fire as they hit the ground or made impact. And the rain was no longer coming down just in the downtown area but on all parts of the city including the uptown area.

A few minutes later the rocks were now falling like a wicked, relentless rain with drops of fiery rocks and water. Every rock that fell smashed into the ground, building, home or other infrastructure with a fiery explosion that consumed everything in its path. The fiery rocks and debris that were pouring down dissolved men, women and children. Those people who were hiding in houses were not safe as the stones tore through concrete, wood and other material to destroy houses and other things in them including people and their pets. Whether it was building blocks or road tar or human flesh, the rocks simply obliterated everything it landed on. In no time at all the casualties began to climb as people in their homes, offices or on the streets died by the rocks. The good news for some was that they died instantly because there was great suffering caused by the meteors. But the bad news was the high casualties that the rocks produced.

The venue of the convention was in the northern end of the uptown part of Mystery River. It was no coincidence that the largest of all the rocks which was a mountain of fire landed on the convention center and buried it on first impact. It took a 3 kilometer diameter part of the city around the center with it down into the ground and thence into the abyss. There were three other such giant mountainous rocks that fell on Happyness with none of them falling on Mystery River. The impact of these rocks shook the foundation of eastern Cretania up to its border with the nation of Atlantis.

The saving grace of the western states of Cretania was that most of the giant rocks that would have leveled the western states fell into the Yellow River close to both shores. They fell in the center of the river from the middle region of the nation as the river slithered southward. The rocks fell from the middle of the river all the way south to the mouth of the river. This rain of giant rocks into the mighty Yellow River created a powerful tsunami whose waters soon arrived on the shores of the eastern and western states. This tsunami caused a powerful flood in the already devastated states of Happyness, Portland and Eastern River. There were also floods in the western states of Shiloh, Calazar and Western River.

The rocks fell as though they were missiles being fired from the heavens by a crazed gigantic power which had determined to wipe Cretania and Cretans from off the face of the earth. At least this was the case in the eastern half of the country where Cretans who lived in this part of the country regretted their residence here. Most citizens had no clue to what was going on and that was the greater tragedy in this nightmare. The heavens were dark like someone had put out the light causing the environment to look like a dark evil cave. The sun didn't come out and the moon was nowhere on this day of darkness and evil nightmare. This first wave as it came down was like a beast unleashing its power as though it was trying to get it over with as fast as possible. But unknown to anyone, including the CMS, this was only the first wave of the destruction. The second wave would soon follow and it promised to unleash an even more brutal calamity. It was like an old man having a bad nightmare that manages miraculously to wake up and rejoices that it was a dream. But he was oblivious to the fact that there was another, a secondary nightmare, about to follow with even deadlier effects.

As predicted by the CMS, the worst-hit states were Happyness, Eastern River and Portland with ground zero being the city of Mystery River in Happyness. Other states on the East including Communitas, North and South Atlantis got off with few or no hits at all. The tsunami and flooding in the aftermath of the falling meteors in the Yellow River affected every state in the country with various degrees of flooding. This was with the exception of the two states at the northern ends of the nation, North Capitol and North Atlantis. All states on the western side of the dichotomy were affected mostly by the tsunami and the flooding. Only the northern-most parts of the Midwest state of Prophétie was untouched by the massive flooding. But the state suffered a slight flooding which soon abated. The shower had devastated all the power-generating plants and disrupted the supply of power to the various distribution grids in the country. There was darkness and despair everywhere and despite what the police and military tried to do, many states were in desperate situations. Gangs and thugs were in control of many suburban areas and metropolitan cities. The 'Nightmare of Darkness,' which had been prophesied by prophets since three decades ago, was finally coming to pass.

At this point which was about seven hours after "The Rains of Mystery River," as the shower was now being called, the armed forces of Cretania was out in full force. Tanks, equipment and artillery which had just been purchased for the army which boasted state-of-the-art technology rolled out of the military bases with full battalion. Every army soldier who was not affected or killed by the disaster was available in their respective bases to move into town and join the effort to restore calm and normalcy. The Navy had also activated all personnel and carriers for the purpose of restoring normalcy on the coasts and avoiding any further damage by the disaster. The Air Force had also activated all personnel and had many of their pilots flying in military jets scouring for areas of devastation and human casualties on land. They had to save as many people as they could, clear the roads and restore transportation systems and set up makeshift health care systems to treat the injured and store dead corpses temporarily. The police were busy guarding corporate buildings, high-value property and similar areas. The law enforcement also protected high net worth individuals and their property to prevent looting and violence.

As the military took control, they reinforced the state of emergency and declared martial law throughout the country. Military roadblocks and checkpoints were put up all over the country. In every state, the military had taken over the political control held by the state governments. The Military Command of the Cretanian Armed Forces and the Cretanian Intelligence Services had convened and declared the military's fifth-highest ranking officer, Lieutenant General Gyros, the Chief of Defense Staff, Chief of Intelligence Services and the Head of State until further notice. The general was not the highest in rank in the Cretanian military but he was the most powerful general in the country, one of the main reasons for that being that he was the highest-ranked of all the favorite soldiers of the president, President Samuel Everlast. His promotion to interim leader of the country also conferred on him the status of a full general.

Not since the days of the Sepsis epidemic about four decades ago had Cretania seen such chaos and pandemonium. All citizens observing these events felt it was 1966 all over again. They believed the devastation of the Sepsis epidemic was here again but this time it was as an astro-geological natural disaster. In Crestar, the newly appointed interim Head of State, General Ferdinand Gyros, was in the presidential office's media room and began to address the nation.

"My fellow citizens of Cretania I salute you in the name of our great country and in the name of God Almighty in the heavens. My name is General Ferdinand Erasmus Gyros. I am the Chief of Defense Staff, Chief of Intelligence Services and the Commanding Officer of the Cretania Military Command which has appointed me the interim Head of State of our great country. I wish to inform you that the government of the former President Samuel Everlast has been officially deposed from office. This is due to the unfortunate circumstances in which we find ourselves because of the current events in our country. As you well know, about 6 to 7 hours ago our nation suffered the greatest tragedy that we have ever witnessed. There has been a massive shower of unidentified cosmic material we believe are meteors and other strange cosmic particles. The debris comprises large rocks and some had the size of small and medium sized mountainous rocks. We have come to understand that this shower is the first of its kind reported not

314

only in this country but also in the world. My government has assembled all our resources and we have our scientists and technicians studying these rocks and particles to determine just what they are. Our people are also trying to understand what has just happened and how best to handle it and prevent it from every happening again. The Emergency forces, the first responders and the health care specialists have not been able to handle the massive numbers of wounded and casualties in this terrible disaster. And so I have instructed the Armed Forces to deploy all resources—engineers, doctors, nurses, and all other needed resources to join in the caring for the wounded and burying the dead. It grieves me to inform you that we have recorded many casualties and are reconciling our records in that regard. I wish to state firmly that my government is on top of all these issues and we are doing all we need to do to put things under control after this terrible disaster. I would also like to warn all criminal elements who may wish to take advantage of this situation to perpetrate any criminal activities to stop and desist from such because we will apprehend and deal ruthlessly with such ungodly elements. Crime and wickedness will never find their place in Cretania. We will restore peace and stability to the nation in due time and until we do we would like to appeal to everyone to stay calm and avoid any restive behavior. On behalf of all the men and women of the Armed Forces of Cretania, I wish the nation and the people of this great nation peace, liberty and prosperity. The Almighty Father will be with us all, Amen."

About 100 miles north of Bethel, the state capital of Prophétie, there was the great mountain, Mont Milieu. It was centrally located in the middle region of the state. At a summit of 20,800 feet, it had a reputation for being one of the most feared highlands in the state. On this day there were a few men who stood on a high elevation in the mountain. These men were looking in the direction of the main areas of impact of the meteor shower in the states of Happyness and Portland. All thirty men seemed to know what was about to happen to the country that fateful day and became witnesses to the events of the day, the beginning of the nightmare. These were the prophets who had received the revelation of what was to happen on that day in Cretania. These men had been forewarned to say nothing to anyone about what was about to happen. Their instruction was to escape to the mountains, witness the events from there and remain there until calm and normalcy returned to the country. From start to finish, these informed men saw it all. They had arrived on the mountains from before the first crow at dawn up till now. It was currently hours into a new day and the prophets were there when the first rays of light appeared in the sky. All the men had escaped the flooding, although it was minor, which had engulfed much of the state. And they stood looking down on the plains of Prophétie from those great heights. Even from that distance they could see the thick dark smoke and fires that shot up from the Eastern States with the worst of the smoke and fires coming from the state of Happyness. Others were focused on the view of Happyness from the distance with the look of shock at the recent events that had just taken place.

To the far right of these observers was another set of witnesses standing at a much higher elevation. The members of this group were also looking towards the east at those places the meteor shower made landfall a few hours ago. These observers were dressed in shiny white garments and were recording everything that had happened in something resembling a notebook. They were hidden from the plain view by the large rocks which surrounded them. And they were totally silent as they documented the detailed record of the events that had just taken, and were still taking, place. A few hours later at about 3 a.m. local time a darkish-gray shadowy object, like a cumulonimbus cloud, appeared in the sky. It came to a stop above the mountains hovering above where the second set of people were standing. As they rose to reach the cloud, the leader of the second group looked down at the prophets and said:

"Do not be alarmed, but the time has come for darkness to seize the land and great shall be the troubles of this great country. Prepare yourselves and your people for what is coming for the power of darkness is upon this beloved nation. Be wise, have understanding and shun ignorance so that you may have a strong chance to survive. Pray the hardest you ever have if you will live to see the end of the storm for the storm will rage indeed. And when the Queen of Thorns rises then know that the eye of the storm has come. She shall wield great power and do unspeakable evil like never before seen in Cretania or even in this generation anywhere in the world. She shall cast down many of the sheep and bring darkness to the land as she seeks to destroy Cretania. Escape to the holy mountains or become like the ants and escape through the mysterious grounds. But the queen shall be betrayed by her own hand and shall be defeated when the Most High shall rise up against her. And when the three weapons shall meet under the golden sun, then the queen shall fall. By the sword, the arrow and fire the queen shall die."

As she finished speaking she turned to look up at the cloud ship as did all the other members of this second group. They all looked up simultaneously and in a second they had disappeared from the vicinity of the mountains with the cloud disappearing as well. The group of prophets were terrified and dumbfounded about what just happened. They all just barely made out

319

the shape of the second group as the chief speaker spoke those words. And none of the prophets ever said a word about the matter since the events of that day.

THE SALVATION OF
NINO STRATA

BY

CHRISTIAN COLOSSUS

END OF PART ONE

TO BE CONTINUED…

END NOTES

About the Author

Christian Colossus (formerly Desmond Ogirri) was born in Lagos, Nigeria and now lives mainly in Canada. One of his primary missions is to expose the truth of salvation so that people may walk in the light rather than the darkness. He became a born again Christian over three decades ago and is a minister, evangelist, teacher of the gospel and author of Christian literature. He teaches and spreads the gospel of Jesus through books and other media. He is a living testimony that with Jesus, who is the almighty God, all things are possible.

Mr. Colossus holds a Bachelor of Science degree in Biochemistry from the University of Maryland College Park in College Park, Maryland, USA. He also holds a Master of Science degree in Bioinformatics from the University of Maryland University College in Adelphi, Maryland, USA.

Christian Colossus also holds undergraduate certificates in Computer Science and a graduate certificate in financial planning. He also holds Canada's Canadian Securities Course (CSC®) financial certification.

Other Books by the Author

1. Salvation 101: An Introduction to Christian Salvation by Christian Colossus

2. Salvation 101: An Introduction to Christian Salvation, 2nd Edition, by Christian Colossus

3. Tales from the Heart: Volume 1: A Collection of Poems, Songs and Short Stories.

Next Book in the Series

The Salvation of Nino Strata, Part 2:

The Rise of the Gyros Clan

The nation of Cretania has been devastated by a natural disaster which many were made to believe was caused by the All-Powerful God, El. General Ferdinand Gyros has taken over the government of the country. In strange twist of fate, the general and his queen lose power but only temporarily. In so many twists and turns, the key players in the battle for this great country rise to power and are positioned by fate to lead their respective sides. Benjamin Strata and his son, Nino, rise to the highest levels of power through political manipulations. Then the Gyros couple regain power after the interim Strata presidency. It is at this point the battle between the two sides head to a climax. The battle for the rich, great and prosperous nation of Cretania heats up in this book. It is a book you must not miss.